## "How dare you call me your fiancée!"

Valeria was furious. Glaring at Bart, she continued, "Of all the goose-brained ideas—you might just as well have called me your mother-in-law!"

"Surely it won't damage your reputation for people to think you're engaged to me," Bart objected. "In fact, it might just add a little luster to your dull life."

"Why, you pompous—"

"Besides, I couldn't think of another thing to say," he concluded regretfully. "I couldn't let that reporter spread the word that we shared a roof unchaperoned. That sort of suggestion always leads to other things we might have shared. How do you think *that* would sit with the governor's council?"

Valeria didn't care. She just wanted to wring his oh-so-appealing neck!

**Emma Goldrick** describes herself as a grandmother first and an author second. She was born and raised in Puerto Rico where she met her husband, a career military man from Massachusetts. His postings took them all over the world, which often led to mishaps—such as the Christmas they arrived in Germany before their furniture. Emma uses the places she's been as backgrounds for her books, but just in case she runs short of settings, this prolific author and her husband are always making new travel plans.

# Pilgrim's Promise

## Emma Goldrick

# Harlequin Books

TORONTO • NEW YORK • LONDON
AMSTERDAM • PARIS • SYDNEY • HAMBURG
STOCKHOLM • ATHENS • TOKYO • MILAN

Original hardcover edition published in 1988
by Mills & Boon Limited

ISBN 0-373-02984-5

Harlequin Romance first edition June 1989

# CHAPTER ONE

'I DON'T think that could be the man,' Valeria said firmly. 'Mr Bart Thomas is his name. I have an appointment to——'

'At the pool,' the desk clerk insisted. 'You're Miss Brewster?'

'Yes, but——'

'But he left word he would be at the pool,' the girl at the desk insisted, and then moved off on other business. Valeria drummed her fingers on the top of the glossy counter and glared around the lobby. The Governor Carver Motor Inn was three floors of brick luxury with a high colonial portico, sitting almost in the centre of Plymouth, but the Brewsters of this world, year-round residents of what had once been Plymouth Plantation, seldom if ever ventured inside.

Val brushed her long hair back from her face. Its wine-dark red sheen framed the golden tan, highlighted the patrician nose, subdued the glaring green eyes. Coming for an appointment and finding her prospective employer at the swimming pool seemed hardly the way to run a business—if that was what he did. She took another look at the embossed card in her hand, and tapped it against the counter. 'Bartholomew Thomas, Esquire.' Whatever that meant. Angrily, she turned on her three-inch heels and clattered across the lobby, following the signs.

The heels were a necessity. They boosted her five foot two inches up to a respectable height. Coupled with her schoolteaching "uniform"—a grey skirt that swirled

5

about her knees, and a white blouse with the tiniest lace frill down the front—it effectively served to disguise her full figure, and added a little dignity to her twenty-six years.

The baking July sun struck her the moment she stepped out of the air-conditioned lobby. The tide was out, and the sharp smell of the mud-flats in Plymouth harbour tickled her nostrils. 'A good day to go fishing,' she muttered angrily as she orientated herself and headed for the pool enclosure.

It was a big, oval pool, with blue water reflecting the bright sun. Only one couple shared the concrete apron. A big, clean-cut man with short blond hair and wide shoulders, perched on a lounge chair that seemed too fragile to bear his weight. The rest of him was covered up by a bikini-clad blonde who cuddled in his lap, her arms around his neck, her lips at his ear. It must have been a dirty joke; they both were in stitches as Valeria steamed up to them and cleared her throat noisily.

'Mr Thomas?' she asked. The man managed to pry himself away from the blonde long enough to look up at her.

'And if I were?'

Valeria looked at his upside-down face. Well-tanned. Whatever 'Mr Thomas, Esquire' did for a living, it hardly kept him indoors—or maybe he owned sun-lamps? Heavy, dark eyebrows, in contrast to his bleached-blond hair. A square sort of face, with just the shadow of a beard-line, as if he had to shave twice a day. Wide-spaced, bright, dark eyes. And an engaging grin, despite the words. If I weren't so darn tired and angry I could like him. Valeria told herself. But——

'If you were, I would have had an appointment with you,' she snapped. 'Since there's some doubt, please excuse me.' She turned on her heel again and started back for the lobby.

'Hey, wait a minute.' The man struggled to get up; the blonde impeded him, objecting. 'Oh, what the hell,' he grumbled. Valeria heard the sound and turned around. He had freed himself by tossing the woman on to an adjacent folding lounge chair, where she sputtered in outrage as he caught up with Val.

'Yes, I'm Thomas,' he chuckled. 'And who might you be?'

'Brewster,' she stated flatly. '*Miss* Brewster. I have a call from my agency stating that you wanted a companion for your daughter.' Valeria wandered a few steps farther toward the pool and stared down at the blonde. The folding lounge chair had done just that—folded up under the impact of her weight, trapping her in its aluminum grip. She was making little squealing noises of panic.

'That's not my daughter.' He caught up with her again and turned her around to face him.

'Maybe not, but she needs rescuing.' Val prodded maliciously.

'Oh, brother,' he muttered as he picked up chair and blonde in one sweep and tried to separate the two by shaking them. He had more grip on aluminum than blonde when the separation occurred. The woman dropped to the concrete on hands and knees and screamed in anger.

'All right,' he muttered as he helped her up and checked for broken bones. The bikini left only the tiniest area unexposed. What he couldn't see he touched. 'Come on, Amelé,' he coaxed as he pushed her over to another chair and assisted her into it. A pat on her scantily covered bottom ended the exercise.

'All right, all right,' the blonde snapped, bending to rub her knees. 'Look what you've done to my——'

'Amelé, this is Miss Brewster,' he interrupted hastily. Valeria could see the gleam in his eyes. 'She's the lady who is going to look after Maria!'

'Wonderful!' The blonde shifted from rage to laughter. It ran tinkling up the scale as she looked Valeria up and down. 'So now we can go to the dance this evening?'

'Now just a minute,' Val sputtered. 'I haven't agreed to *anything* yet. I was told you wanted a companion, not a baby-sitter. I'm not at all sure I want——'

'Go get dressed.' Thomas instructed the blonde. 'Miss Brewster and I would like to have a little talk.'

'I think, under the circumstances, that Mrs Thomas ought to remain,' Val said stiffly.

'Now talk your way out of that one,' Amelé giggled as she wrapped a towel around herself and headed towards the lobby doors. 'Try a little of that courtroom charm, darling.'

He watched the blonde wiggle her way across the pool area and through the door, and then turned back to Valeria. 'There isn't any Mrs Thomas,' he explained hastily. 'At least, not at the moment. Why don't you and I——' He stopped talking long enough to rub himself down with a beach towel and slide his legs into a pair of silver track-suit bottoms. 'Why don't you and I step into the lounge and talk over a drink?'

It was hardly an invitation. One of his big paws locked up her wrist in a death-grip, and she found herself being towed across the concrete apron of the pool and into the air-conditioned shade of the lobby.

The Thirsty Pilgrim Lounge was as empty as the pool area. The tourists and commercial travellers who lodged at the inn were already about their business. Thomas led her to a far table, and the two waitresses on duty had the sense to leave them alone until called. He ushered her into a seat, and then sprawled out on a tiny chair across from her, with his back to the room.

'Drink?'

'Lemonade,' she answered. 'Tell me about Maria.' Her hands nervously played with the little silver brooch that fastened the neck of her blouse.

'In good time,' he insisted, raising one finger as a summons. 'First, tell me something about yourself. I asked for the toughest female teacher in the high school. I find it hard to believe you're the one.'

'Believe it.' She managed, with a few economical feminine movements, to straighten her blouse and get her hair back where it belonged. I should have braided it, she thought. I should have had it cut! Wasn't that the old-fashioned signal of spinsterhood, when a woman gave up the chase, had her hair cut, started to wear mob caps and became a maiden aunt? A little grin twitched at the corner of her mouth.

'Age?'

'Well, really!' she snorted. 'I'm old enough to be a child's companion. I've been teaching for five years. And I'm only interested in a temporary job—something to tide me over the summer vacation. Now, tell me about you.'

His eyes narrowed. She could see he hadn't expected her to take over the interview. Stuffed shirt, she told herself. And what was that about 'courtroom manners'? A lawyer? Where could Mrs Thomas be?

'Yes, I understand that part of it, Miss Brewster. That's just what I need. Someone to help us over the rough spots this summer until I can make more permanent arrangements.'

The drinks came, terminating *that* line of questioning. Valeria sniffed at hers before sampling it. Too many resort-lounges were serving their lemonade out of a can these days. Out of the corner of her eye she could see Thomas slug down a neat whisky. He shrugged his shoulders and turned on the charm.

Those big dark eyes, she warned herself. There's the danger. A girl could fall into them and drown. His magnificent baritone voice roamed the musical scale, but her mind was already adrift, and she caught one word out of ten. 'Daughter...mother no longer with us...work in Boston...need a suburban environment for the child to grow up in...full care for eight weeks——' And he named a sum of money that battered its way into her wandering mind and left her choking on her drink.

'The drink isn't satisfactory?' He leaned across the table and took the glass from her suspiciously. 'I never could understand lemonade,' he added as he set the glass down in front of her again.

'There's nothing wrong with the drink,' she gasped. 'Nothing. I—I'm sorry about your wife. I thought the young lady——'

'Not at all,' he chuckled. 'Amelé Poitras is a—friend of mine—nothing more. Now, about yourself?'

'I—live here in Plymouth.' She steadied herself, folded her hands and put them on the edge of the table. 'I teach social studies at the regional high school.'

'Family?'

'None,' she sighed.

'Sorry,' he apologised curtly. Those eyes of his were boring holes in her, searching out every secret that might be read on her mobile face. She schooled herself more closely.

'No need. It all happened years ago. Why would you choose Plymouth to come to, Mr Thomas?'

'Bart,' he insisted. 'Call me Bart. Well, Plymouth is only forty miles from the city, with a good interconnecting highway system. Did I make a mistake?'

'I guess it all depends,' Valeria sighed. 'Plymouth, Massachusetts, America's home town. It's become a tourist resort, you know. Have you found a house?'

'Yes.' He toasted her with his refilled glass. 'A little place down on the shore near Cobbs Hollow. But it needs some work done on it. Now what?'

For the second time in as many minutes, Valeria was choking over her lemonade. A little place down on the shore near Cobbs Hollow! What a laugh that was. An area of huge and vast expanses of close-cut green grass, running from Sandwich Street to the shoreline. A 'little place' must be one with less than fourteen rooms!

She wiped the tears from her eyes and took two deep breaths. 'What was it you said you did for a living?' she enquired cautiously.

'I thought I mentioned that. I'm a corporate lawyer. I have my own firm in the financial district in Boston. Now, about your ability to handle my thirteen-year-old daughter Maria?'

'I don't see that as a problem.' Valeria sat up and offered her most prim expression. 'I handle five classes a day, twenty-six students per class—and they *all* have problems. What makes you believe that Maria has more difficulties than most children?'

Bart Thomas drummed his fingers on the table, as if debating how much she needed to be told. 'My daughter was raised by my wife, in Beverly Hills——'

'California?' she interrupted. He gave her a wry smile.

'Beverly Hills, California,' he agreed. 'Movie stars and the fast life. That sort of thing. And now she's come to live with me. It's a world of change. Both she and I have to make some sort of compromise in our life-styles.'

Yes, Val thought, and I can imagine which one of you is going to make the most changes! From Hollywood to a corporate lawyer? Poor child. 'You say you lost your wife, Mr Thomas? Illness or accident?'

'Divorce court,' he answered glumly. 'Why?'

'Because, however it happened, your daughter will be affected by it. Your—former wife is——'

'About to marry a movie producer,' he snapped. 'And I don't care for that line of questioning. I'm not sure you'll do, Miss Brewster.'

'I was about to say the same thing myself,' Valeria commented as she pushed away from the table, glaring at him.

'Just a minute.' He leaned forward across the tiny table. 'Let me finish what I have to say, at least.'

She shrugged her shoulders and settled back into the chair.

'I'm not sure you'll do,' he repeated, 'but I haven't had any other takers.' He sounded as if he were stating a palpable falsehood. As if it were impossible that a dozen or more applicants were not pounding at his door.

'Maybe you could try Miss Poitras,' Vas suggested.

'Don't be silly,' he sighed. 'Amelé has certain—limited—uses. Maria can't stand her. But then, Maria can't stand practically anybody, it seems. How about a compromise—what the devil *is* your Christian name?'

'Valeria.' She offered it softly, not really wanting him to hear. There was something about this whole affair that puzzled her. The man had all the attributes of perfection; a perfectly *impossible* creature. And yet, from time to time, for a brief second or two, a real person seemed to peer out at her through those dark, passionate eyes.

'Valeria.' He rolled it around on his tongue. 'Unusual. Talking to you is like trying to swim in a bowl of jelly, Valeria Brewster. How about a compromise? We both put aside our doubts for a few days and work to Maria's benefit?'

Val ducked her head to get away from his penetrating stare, and rhythmically tapped a finger into the palm of her other hand as she thought. So far, the only thing going for him was that absolutely tremendous sum of money he had mentioned. It could do a lot. A new roof for her little house; a memorial stone for Gran. Maybe even a new—well, a less well-used—car to take the place of the wreck she drove. Scratch that. A better photocopier was what she really needed. It was impossible to crank out the leaflets she required for *all* her little protest campaigns on the piece of junk she now had.

But—the big word. Suppose sweet little Maria didn't take to Miss Valeria Brwester? Out of the corner of her eye she saw him signal for the waitress again, and a third glass was in front of him. Strange. He watched her like a hawk, and his hand trembled when he picked up the glass. He was either a confirmed alcoholic, or this whole affair was of some importance to him and was shaking his iron nerve!

'If you're willing,' she said in her soft, sweet voice, 'then I am—temporarily. But it will all depend on how Maria feels, you understand. I brought some references.'

He seemed to sag, and then pull himself up again as he picked up the envelope she offered and ran through the papers. 'One doctor, one principal, one police chief? You know the chief well?'

'He—seems to think so,' she chuckled. 'We transact a great deal of business together, Chief Peterson and I. You're not going to read them?'

'Later,' he returned. 'More lemonade?'

'I think I'd rather meet your daughter.' she proposed.

He got up slowly, a doubtful expression on his face, as if he would prefer her signature on a contract *before* she met the little girl. The thought earned a smile. He came around the table to hold her chair while she rose. Valeria looked up at him, and the smile died. He seemed to stretch upward for ever. She hadn't noticed that earlier. A square, Scandinavian face, full of strengths. Those dark eyes and eyebrows. Square shoulders funnelling down to a narrow waist and hips. A very great deal of man, she told herself. Pompous, perhaps. Troubled. But still a great deal of man.

He took her arm and urged her back out into the lobby, where he sent a bellboy to search for the child. 'We can wait at the pool,' he suggested. 'It seems to be empty. And I wouldn't want you to have to meet her in her bedroom.'

'No,' Valeria agreed, and then wondered why she had said such a thing. Why *not* meet the child in a bedroom? What in the world could possibly be *that* wrong?

'And another thing,' he hurried to interject. 'I have to go back to Boston tonight. I would like you to stay here with Maria until Monday.'

'You mean you want me to jump in over my head?' She tugged him to a stop. 'And try to control a potentially uncooperative child in a downtown motel? Nonsense!'

'I can't help it,' he insisted. 'It's business—with the state.'

'For a whole weekend? And a dance included?' She let him feel the sharp side of her tongue on that one, and he flinched.

'The Charity Ball,' he said stiffly. 'More business gets accomplished at these functions than during a normal work-week. And I didn't intend your duties to include criticising my life-style, Miss Brewster.'

'Oh, dear, no,' she returned sarcastically. 'So your daughter and I will go back to my house and spend the weekend there. If she's willing to go *anywhere* with me, that is.'

He ran a hand through his hair in a nervous gesture, and then shrugged his shoulders. 'All right, we'll do it your way. Here she comes.'

The pair of them were about four feet from the edge of the pool. Valeria turned to watch, and almost swallowed her tongue. 'Oh, my God,' the big man beside her muttered.

The child, if that were the right word, who came through the door was about five feet four—at least a couple of inches taller than Valeria, over-developed for her age, and weighed down by chubbiness. She was dressed in a pair of tattered grey denims and a man's loose shirt, the tails of which reached to her knees. As she strutted toward them, some of the details became more obvious. Rouge spots on her cheeks, eyes heavy with mascara, and orange lipstick outlined her full mouth. But it was the hair that took the prize.

There was no way to determine what its real colour might be. At the moment it was dyed a bilious green. And scattered tufts had been soaked in some thickener and teased upward in the form of little spikes, three across the front of her head and two in the back.

'Thirteen years old, you said?' Valeria whispered. The child looked like earth-mother. Overweight, over-developed, overdressed. A teenager making a protest statement!

The man beside her took a deep breath and muttered half a dozen words in some Slavic language as he struggled to control himself. 'Yes, thirteen,' he grated. The girl came to a halt in front of them and stared Valeria up and down.

'Maria,' her father said, 'This is Miss Brewster. She's going to look after you for a few days.'

'I don't think so,' Maria returned. 'What are you staring at?' Valeria was staring at the child's bare feet.

Valeria raised her head slowly, returning the insolent inspection she herself had just received. There was no doubt about it, the child's feet were black. Not painted—just dirty.

'I was just thinking,' Val said softly. 'I looked like that once—on the day I stole all my father's watercolour paints. I was supposed to be an Indian in the school play. What are you supposed to be?'

Maria's cheeks turned red, and anger glittered in eyes that matched her father's. Dark, deep anger. 'I'm not *supposed* to be anything,' she snapped. 'I'm just *me*. You small-town people just don't know!'

'About being *you*? I suppose you're right,' Val agreed amiably. 'Is that any reason why we can't spend a day or two together while your father finishes up some important work?'

'Hah!' The child broke out a grin that was more teeth than good humour. 'With a goody two-shoes like you?'

'Maria,' her father cautioned.

'I haven't heard that phrase in years,' Valeria chuckled. 'Goody two-shoes! You're more old-fashioned than I thought, young lady.'

It was the straw that broke the camel's back. Valeria could read the trouble in the girl's eyes even before it came her way. She backed up a few inches until her heels were balanced on the edge of the pool, and waited. Three years in a row as the captain of the University of Massachusetts swimming team, and, no mean actress herself, her quick mind had already decided that a great deal of water, applied thoroughly, might be a solution to the present impasse.

So when Maria ran at her, making good speed for a child of her bulk, planted both hands in Valeria's stomach and pushed, Val managed a passable scream in pseudo-panic, making sure that both the child's hands were locked in her own, and fell backward into the pool, dragging the girl with her.

Bart Thomas was caught completely off guard. Val came to the surface easily, and checked to see the man struggling out of his track suit. The child was an adequate swimmer, and now it was time for Act Two.

'Help!' Valeria called softly, splashing her way to the middle of the pool where Maria was trying to keep out of the way. 'Help!' With seeming awkwardness she grabbed the child's shoulders in panic, and forced the girl down underwater, her hands slipping from the child's shoulders to her hair.

It could hardly have been more than a minute before Bart Thomas came arching over the pair of them in a clean dive, and reversed his field to come up behind Maria. But in that short a time Valeria had managed to duck the girl four times, massage her hair and cheeks vigorously, and then float away on her back in a lazy stroke that allowed her to coast to the ladder.

The two Thomases were close behind her, the one angry, the other solicitous, as they offered help up the ladder. Help of which Valeria had no need at all.

'I'm sorry,' Bart muttered. 'I'm really sorry.'

'No need to be,' Valeria answered as she swung her heavy mane of hair over one shoulder and began to wring it out. 'Accidents will happen. Won't they, Maria?'

The girl looked at her warily, not sure about the word, unwilling to take any more risks with her visibly angry father, plainly shaken at the wrong turn her plot had taken. 'I—yes——' the child stammered. 'Accidents will happen.'

'Come to my room,' he commanded. 'You both look like drowned rats.' He spared a hand for each of them, towing them along into the main section of the inn and down the corridor to a corner room. An interconecting door led to the room next door. He gestured them through.

'This is Maria's room. I have a suspicion that some of her clothing might fit you—approximately. That pool is chlorinated. I recommend you both take a hot shower, and then we'll talk.' He shut the door behind them with just the touch of a slam to emphasise the words.

The girl stalked to the bed and threw herself down on it, paying no attention to her soaked condition. 'A shower is a good idea,' Valeria told her. 'Shall I go first?'

'I don't care *what* you do,' the child responded angrily. 'You don't appear to be all that dumb. Didn't you get the message out there? I was happier before you came, and I'll be overwhelmed after you leave. So why don't you?'

'Is that the way you talked to your mother?' Valeria walked over to the side of the bed. Poor kid. The thought ran through her mind over and over, like a circular tape in a video machine. Poor, poor kid.

The girl sat up and glared at her. 'You're not my mother,' she snapped. 'My mother is—pretty. She makes movies. She'd not some ugly old—baby-sitter.'

'You could be pretty, too,' Val commented, firmly overlooking all the other statements.

'I could not,' Maria grumbled. 'I'm not blind, you know. My mother told—she—oh, go get your shower!'

Valeria held the eye contact for a second, and then the child broke away, flushing. *My mother is pretty— I'm not. I'm not blind!* Another set of phrases to roll over in her mind as Val walked over to the door that led to the bathroom. *I'm not pretty.* How would a thirteen-year-old girl really know that—have it so fixed in her mind—unless someone told her so, and more than once?

The thought continued to bother her as Val shed her soaked clothing and stepped into the warm shower. The steam rose around her, wrapping her up in comforting warm arms as she puzzled over the man and the girl and the future. The little bar of soap was typically American-hotel size. Too big to forget; not big enough to really work up a lather. Disgusted, she set it back on the tiny porcelain holder and let the warm water take over.

Five minutes later, her bronzed body blush-red from the heat, she stepped out of the shower. Maria was bent over the hot rail. The girl straightened up and took one quick look before Val swathed herself in one of the larger bath-towels.

'Oh!' The girl clapped her hand over her mouth and backed away.

'Oh?' Val let the friendly little smile form on her face.

'You're not—I thought you were one of those—you're not ugly at all,' the girl stammered. 'You have lovely hair.'

'Why, thank you,' Val chuckled. 'I've been meaning to have it cut. Like yours, maybe.'

'Oh no, don't do that,' Maria returned seriously. 'I only do mine this way because my dad doesn't like it. What colour is that?'

My grandmother used to call it wine-red,' Val said as she snatched up another towel and began to rub.

'You have a grandmother?' There were acres of yearning in the simple question.

'Not any longer,' Val sighed. 'She died some years ago. How about *your* grandmother?'

'I don't know,' the girl muttered, and then she put on her "brave" face and spoke up. 'She don't like me, either. I was only playing baseball in her yard and the ball broke

the window and she screamed at me and called Dad and
he came to get me and——' The child ran out of breath.
She gobbled a mouthful of air, and then said 'You got
a nice figure, too. I wish I could have had one like that.'

'You should have seen me when I was thirteen,' Val
commented solemnly. 'I weighed more then than I do
now, and I had pimples besides! Why don't you hop
into the shower? I think your dad might want to say
something more to us.'

'I brought you something you might be able to wear.'
Maria changed the subject quickly, pointing to a towelling robe she had laid across the hot-bar. Valeria snatched
it up, looked at the child speculatively, and headed for
the door. It's obvious that the girl doesn't want to display
herself to me or anyone else, she thought. Somebody
has damaged this child mentally, and made a nervous
wreck out of her!

Twenty minutes later the two of them came back into
the first bedroom. Bart Thomas, encased in a pair of
razor-sharp trousers and an open-necked sports shirt,
rose from his chair by the window.

'What a difference a shower makes,' he commented.
'If you'll give me your clothing, Miss Brewster, the motel
claims they can have it cleaned and dried in thirty
minutes.'

Valeria nodded, handing him the bundle she carried.
He weighed it in one of those big hands, and grinned.
'Not much to it, is there?' he chuckled as he strode to
the door. The bellboy was standing outside in the corridor, waiting.

And that, Valeria thought, is how the rich get service.
Instantaneous, if you're rich enough. I didn't know that
lawyering paid *that* much money! That little smile
crinkled at one corner of her mouth again as she looked

over at her partner in crime. Washed, Maria's hair had been reduced to its naturally dull brown. Something that a few shampoos and some considerable brushing would be bound to improve, Val told herself.

There was something else that had changed, too. Although the child was still visibly overweight, her proportions had diminished considerably, bespeaking a considerable amount of padding that had been removed! She still retained more than the expected amount of baby fat, but the grossness was gone. Val's smile turned to a wide grin. Maria ducked her head and turned away from the pair of them. Bart Thomas sauntered back from the door, hands in pockets, looking like a boy who wanted to whistle but didn't dare. Valeria caught herself in the middle of one of her own typical mental forays, comparing people she had just met with recalcitrant students. Bart Thomas was like—no, he wasn't either! No bashful schoolboy lurked under his smooth, tanned skin. This one was a stalking leopard, all sleek and smooth and deadly!

'I'm afraid the plan won't work, Mr Thomas,' Val told him. 'Your daughter just doesn't like me. I think you had better revert to Plan One—let Miss Poitras look after her while you tend to your business.'

'Good lord, not that!' The child was startled beyond reason, whirling around to confront them both. Her father was almost as startled as she, but managed to hide his response behind a grim face. 'You can't dump me on Amelé, Dad! She's—you can't!'

'Well, I don't really have any choice,' he replied sternly. 'I can't take you back to Boston with me. So, as Miss Brewster suggests, if you don't want to stay with *her*, it will have to be Amelé.'

The girl thought it over for a moment or two, glaring at them both, then she whirled around and let them have the back of her as she stared out the window.

'I would have to stay with—with Miss Brewster for the whole weekend?'

'Yes.'

'We'll go to my house,' Valeria explained. 'And it's only two days. You can help me take care of my dog. Your dad will be back on Monday.' She stared at the man. 'Won't he?' she demanded in her best prim schoolteacher's voice.

'Well, I had thought that——' He wanted to qualify the statement in some way, but knew he was caught, hoist with his own petard. 'Yes,' he said gruffly. 'Monday, before noon, love.'

'Oh, Dad!' The child whirled around again and hugged him. 'I won't mind. Not for just a couple of days. And then we can move into our new house, and everything will be——'

'And everything will be fine,' he promised gently, stroking the still-wet brush of hair. His eyes met Valeria's over the head bent into his chest. There was some enigmatic challenge in them. Some message that *she* could not interpret. 'I'm going to order us a snack,' he continued in that deep bass voice. 'And make a couple of long-distance telephone calls. You two amuse each other for a while.'

Valeria stood in the middle of the room, hands on hips, and watched him. He had not even *contemplated* an objection from either of them, but just walked out and closed the door behind him.

'Well!' she said, and threw up her hands, laughing.

'Yes,' his daughter agreed. 'He's like that. What can I do about my hair?'

'Brush it,' Val said firmly. 'Brush it, one hundred strokes. It will grow back, you know.'

The girl measured her for an endless moment, and then started to move toward the interconnecting door. 'I don't mind putting up with you for a while,' she said fiercely, 'but don't get no ideas about my dad! He and my mother—they're going to get back together any day now! So you don't have to make goose-eyes at him!'

'Goose-eyes?' Valeria suppressed the giggle as she followed the child into the next room.

# CHAPTER TWO

FINDING the house was no easy matter. Bart Thomas made four false starts before he came upon a postman willing to point him in the direction of Little Pond. By that time it was four o'clock on Monday afternoon. His foot came down too heavily on the accelerator as he tried to make up for his self-imposed noon deadline. A siren sounded behind him almost immediately.

After the long discussion with the State policemen, it was four-thirty before he made the right turn off Summer Street and pulled up beside the little wooden two-storey cottage.

He was almost too tired to move out of the car. The twenty-four-hour Cancer Telethon, followed by after-midnight hours at the Charity Ball, had left him little time to tidy up all the cases in his personal file, and no time at all for sleep. He examined the little house with half-closed eyes.

A Cape Cod cottage, Valeria's house was one of those border-line cases, neither old or new. In a town founded in 1620, a house built in 1816 outside the city limits was not much to talk about. The city had grown outward since those days, and now extended beyond the little en-clave. Trimmed in white, its weathered clapboard shingles wore the patina of age. Small rooms and low ceilings preserved the heat from open fireplaces; all the plumbing had been added on, most of it outside. Small leaded windows sparkled at the world, giving the house a smiling appearance. A white picket fence shut it off from the street. Rambling roses surmounted the fence and perfumed the air. An elderly neighbour hung on the gate just across the street. He could hear the sound of voices and followed them around the side of the house to the small garden in its rear. A very ancient German schnauzer, its black coat liberally sprinkled with grey, raised its head, sniffed the air in his direction, and went back to sleep.

The two women were sharing a drink around a round white outdoor table in the shade of an old maple tree. *Lemonade,* he told himself wryly. They were both in one-piece bathing-suits. His daughter seemed overly neat, hair burnished brown, and no cosmetics in sight.

'He's not going to come,' the girl grumbled as she looked at her wristwatch.

'He'll come.' The older finished her drink and stood up.

'But it's four-thirty already, and he said noon.'

'Men are like that,' Valeria chuckled. 'They invented time, and they work it for all it's worth.' She stretched and took a deep breath before collapsing in her chair again.

Bartholomew Thomas, Esquire, felt as if something had just hit him in the pit of his stomach. All the way down from Boston, driving his Mercedes with the roof open, he had dissected the dozen beautiful women presented to him at the Ball, and savoured each. Not once had he given a thought to the "schoolteacher" who was watching over his daughter.

And now, standing in the dappled sunlight as she stretched, he realised what a mistake he had made. The woman's slim, supple figure was neat enough to grace any occasion. Her dark red hair was caught up in a coronet around her head, and glistened in the late afternoon sun. And when she smiled, her face became a thing of beauty. If school teachers had been like this when *he* was in school, he assured himself, he would have learned a great deal more than he had!

'So we'll see a little of Plymouth tomorrow after we do our jogging?' Valeria questioned.

'If he don't come,' Maria muttered. 'Why do they call it America's home town?'

'That's just a Chamber of Commerce thing,' Val laughed. 'You know the Pilgrims came across the ocean from England and landed here to start the first permanent colony? Surely you've heard about that? Even in the California school system.'

'Wasn't there some little earlier settlement down in Virginia?' Bart Thomas asked as he sauntered over in their direction. The dog manufactured one sharp bark.

'Daddy?' Maria yelled as she dropped her lemonade glass and stood up. Caution was written in all the angles of her body. He tossed the jacket he had been carrying on to the nearest chair and hugged his daughter. The child held herself stiffly, unforgiving, until the man released her.

'That bit about settlers in Jamestown was just a ploy by the Virginia State legislature,' Valeria interjected, trying to break the mood with a little humour. 'Plymouth is the earliest continually inhabited settlement north of Florida.'

'Well——' de drawled, shuddering. 'It's a little chilly down here, isn't it? How are you, Miss Brewster?'

'Mr Thomas,' she acknowledged stiffly. 'You're late. Would you like some lemonade?'

'Good lord, no,' he responded. 'Something more— lively, perhaps.'

'I have some of my grandmother's elderberry wine.' She rose gracefully from her chair, a querying look on her face. 'It's four years old. A very good age for elderberry?'

'I—well, if that's what you have——' he said wryly.

'How gracious of you,' she muttered as she stalked by him and went into the house. What a terrible personality, she thought as her hands busied themselves by the kitchen window. He couldn't convince a jury of nuns that the Bible is a holy book!

Bart Thomas dropped into the middle of the outdoor sofa-swing, and rocked himself a couple of times with the toe of one shoe, yawning.

'So have you had a good time, Maria?'

His daughter slumped down in the opposite chair and rested both elbows on the little table. 'Around here?' she grumbled. 'You know they take the sidewalks in at eight o'clock at night?'

'So what did you do?' Somehow, he told himself, I've got to break down Maria's reserve. She can't go on for ever dreaming of Beverly Hills. Her loving little mother was quick enough to get rid of her when marriage offered. Or was it perhaps her new beau's command?

'We went for a run. Would you believe that? She jogs every day. Five miles. Crazy.' The girl stroked her hair self-consciously.

'A lot of people are into jogging,' he chuckled. 'And then what?'

'And then we went down to see the Mayflower. It isn't even real! It's an imitation. I don't believe any of it's real. Ucchh!' The girl made a face and looked up scornfully as Valeria came out with a tray. 'Boring,' Maria continued. 'All boring.'

Valeria smiled as she filled a glass and leaned down to hand it to Bart. 'There aren't any boring *places*,' she mused gently. 'Only boring *people*. I thought you had a good time on the ship.'

'Yeah, well I did, until the guards made me stop climbing in the rigging. And it's a fake ship.'

'My God,' her father muttered. They both looked over at him. He swallowing hard. 'This is wine?'

'Well, Gran really did like her drinks a little strong,' Valeria offered in apology. 'Would you prefer——?'

'No, this will do,' he interrupted. 'I just wasn't expecting—well, it will do very well.' He took another sip, and then downed the whole glass.

'It's not really a fake ship,' he lectured his daughter. 'Wooden ships don't last for ever, you know. And when it was decided to make a copy of the Mayflower for a movie, they came as close to the original as they could. It's a very good thing. Makes you think of our origins, Maria.'

'Ha,' the girl snorted. '*Our* relatives didn't come over from the Old Country until 1919.' Bart Thomas took another tug at his refilled glass and became considerably more mellow than before.

'I know that,' he reprimanded. 'But Miss Brewster here—that's an old Yankee name if ever I heard one. Half the town is named Brewster. And the other half Winslow, I think—our Miss Brewster here, she doesn't know that.'

'Not that bad,' Valeria corrected. 'Besides, I don't come from *that* branch of the Brewster family.'

'So what else did you do?' he probed. He shifted his weight to bring both legs up on the swing, and rested his head against the pillows piled at one end. His glass was empty again. Valeria filled it.

'Not much,' the child said stonily. 'Your Miss Brewster here writes things and prints them on a photocopier.' His Miss Brewster leaned over and refilled his glass one more time with her fingers crossed. A job is a job is a job, she told herself, and I can't afford to lose this one before it even gets started. Somehow I have to disguise my little—hobby!

'Interesting,' he muttered as he finished off the glass in one gulp. 'What about?'

'About the nuclear power plant,' his daughter yelled at him.

'Thas' good,' he managed. 'We all needa support our nuclear power plants. Need the elec—the elec——' His mind and mouth gave out at the same time. His empty glass dropped on to the thick grass at about the same time that his eyes closed.

'Well, I'll be darned,' his daughter said, concerned. 'I've never seen him *that* way before.'

'He must have had a hard weekend,' Valeria offered sympathetically as she held the almost-empty bottle up to the light of the sun and measured it. 'Of course, Gran's wine has a very high alcohol content. She fortified it with something. Brandy, I think. She put this up the year she died.'

His daughter was too sharp for excuses. 'I think he's drunk,' she said, sidling closer to inspect her sprawling parent. 'And he wasn't when he came in, was he?'

'No, I guess not,' Val chuckled. 'Oh, well. Saves explanations.'

'About nuclear power plants?' The girl gave her a thousand-year-old shrewd look of comprehension. 'You're not really *for* them, are you?'

'Of course not,' Val agreed, her happy mood turning sour. 'My classroom is exactly two and half miles from that nuclear pile. Any sort of accident, no matter how minor, would wipe out our school! The plant's closed for safety improvements, and I want to see it *stay* that way. Closed, I mean!'

'Wow,' Maria replied. 'So why don't you go over there and put up a picket line?'

'I did that last week,' Valeria sighed. 'It wasn't too smart.'

'What happened?' Maria's round face showed its first sign of interest since the pair of them had met.

'Well, it was a strategic mistake to begin with,' Valeria recounted. 'We wanted to make a statement by closing the plant. Which was pretty stupid, since it was already closed. So, as we had come that far, we set up a picket line. Set down, I should say. There were about twenty-five of us. We sat down on the access road.'

'And then what happened?'

'Not much,' Val admitted. 'Nobody came or went all morning, but at noon there was a party of officials. So we did our thing. Signs and chants and a little wild dancing. And that ended that.'

'What do you mean—*ended* that?'

'The State police came along and arrested the whole bunch of us for trespassing, and we couldn't find a single lawyer in the city to take us on, so we spent the night in jail.'

'Like wow! Maria exclaimed in delight. 'In jail! Now that's what I call protesting! Wait until my dad hears about that!'

'Now that's a problem,' Valeria sighed. 'I really *do* need the money, Maria. And if your dad hears about my—er—hobbies, I'm sure he'll find some quick way to dispense with my services.'

'Yeah,' the girl agreed glumly. 'Leaving me in the hands of that—Amelé Poitras. Well—so I won't tell him——' She looked up at Valeria's wide grin and matched it. 'Not right now, that is.'

Valeria, who knew a blackmailer when she saw one, nodded as she did her best to make Bart comfortable on the swaying couch. His shoes came off easily enough, and his belt loosened, but she could do nothing with the sombre tie he wore, and ended up by stretching him out and covering his face with her old straw hat against the last slanted rays of sunlight.

'So you'll have a criminal record.' The girl pursued her target relentlessly but softly, lest her father wake up and hear.

'Not me,' Valeria chuckled. 'I escaped the heavy hand of the law on a technicality.'

'Now that's something I need to know about,' Maria insisted. 'I may make a career out of protesting. Tell me about the technicality.'

'I can't give you a legal explanation,' Val said as she stepped back to admire her work. He wasn't snoring—but his mouth was half-open, and there was a slight whistle to his exhaling. The worry lines had already faded, leaving a more boyish expression on his face. Something about his relaxed face caught at her heart. She turned around to the girl.

'The truth is that Judge Cornwall used to be a beau of my mother's years ago. I don't think even the prosecutor knew what the grounds were, but the judge dismissed the case. Now, how about you and I doing something in the kitchen?'

'Doing something in the kitchen?' Maria asked scornfully. 'My mother never did anything in the kitchen, so why should I? To tell the truth, I'm not sure she even knew where it was. We had a big apartment, you know. A condo.'

'Well, there's no time like the present to improve your knowledge.' Valeria teased. 'C'mon, chum.'

'Do we hafta wait for Dad to wake up?' Maria was rubbing her eyes, although it was hardly five-thirty in the afternoon. While Valeria had busied herself with home-made clam chowder, a tossed salad, and not-so-home-made biscuits, the girl had held herself aloof, as if things of the kitchen were beyond her. But as Val worked she noticed that Maria's eyes were following her every move, and when the succulent smell of chowder filled the kitchen the child's nose twitched.

'No, I don't suppose we *hafta*,' Valeria smiled. 'But just in case, why don't you run out there and see if he's still sleeping?'

The girl was back in a flash. 'Still sleeping,' she reported disgustedly as she inhaled the kitchen odours hungrily.

'So we'll eat without him,' Val decided. 'Help me set the table.'

There was no holding back. Maria was clumsy but willing. And when the chowder and steaming hot biscuits were served she spooned up in the best New England tradition.

'I think I ate too much,' Val groaned as they swept the plates clean and leaned back. 'Blueberry pie?'

'I ain't got no—I don't have any more room,' Maria sighed, patting her stomach. 'And we didn't save any chowder for Dad!'

'No,' Val chuckled, 'Rudolph gets the left-overs.'

'Your dog likes clam chowder?'

'Why not. He's a lifelong member of the family, and if that's an accusation, we're both guilty. You ate your share—and then some,' Valeria laughed. 'I could make your dad a liver and onion sandwich. But I don't think he'd appreciated us waking him up just to eat home cooking.' And it's been a whole hour without the child reminding me what her most perfect mother does or doesn't do, Val thought. Glory be! She managed to struggle away from the table and began collecting the dirty dishes. Maria hung back.

'Why don't you go sit with your father? He might wake up and forget where he is,' Val suggested. The girl smiled at the idea, and hurried out into the gathering twilight. Occasionally, as she worked at the sink, Val looked out the window into the back yard. Maria was hunched up in a chair just across from the swing where her father lay sleeping, leaning forward a little as if trying to share the man's dreams.

Valeria dried her hands, untied her apron, and went to the screen door to watch. I wonder just what I've got myself into, she asked herself. The girl is trying to absorb all her father's love and attention but refuses to let go of her memories of her mother. Just what is she thinking? And Bart? Gran Brewster's wine was potent, but could four glasses put a grown man to sleep like that? They need each other, those two. I wonder if they know it? Or if they both need someone else?

Gran Brewster's wine? There was a little breeze blowing in through the open door, heavy with the smells of Gran's roses. It brought too many memories. She could remember neither her father or mother. Grandpa had gone ten years since and her memory clothed him with her childhood memories. But Gran—sweet, ornery, lovable Gran had died but eighteen months past, leaving Valeria firmly committed to the paths that Gran had laid out. Never suffer a fault in silence! It might well have been graven over the kitchen door. She shook herself back to attention with a quirky little smile at the corners of her mouth. Rudolph staggered up, shook himself, and took refuge in his favourite corner for the night.

The telephone rang.

'Is this the Brewster girl who's taking care of Maria?' Sharp, penetrating, high tones, flavoured with just a shade of condescension. Amelé Poitras, at a guess. Valeria admitted to all her sins.

'Then is Bart there?' Val stuck out her tongue at the mouthpiece of the telephone, and admitted that His Mightiness was indeed present.

'Get him to the telephone. Hurry up!'

'I can't do that,' Val said gently. 'He's—indisposed.'

'Indisposed? What the hell does that mean?' the other girl snapped down the line.

Val moved the earpiece away from her ear. 'Indisposed. It means he's not available to come to the telephone, Miss Poitras.'

'So you *do* know *who* I am,' the other woman shrilled. 'Do you know *where* I am?'

'No, I'm afraid I don't,' Val chuckled. It was turning out to be an old Abbot and Costello routine, and she might as well carry it to its end. 'Do *you* know where *I* am?'

'No, I don't,' Amelé grumbled. 'The address isn't listed in the telephone book!'

'Thank goodness for that,' Val sighed as she gently hung up the phone.

'Who was that?' The screen door slammed as Maria wandered back into the kitchen.

'Believe me, you wouldn't want to know,' Val muttered. 'Hey, I have a little work to do. Why don't you settle for a bath and a little television and an early bed?'

'You must be kidding,' the child complained. 'It's hardly seven o'clock. I don't go to bed before eleven or twelve. Not ever!'

'If you say so,' Val chuckled. 'Me, I go to bed earlier than—lord, what are we going to do about your father?'

'Don't ask me,' the child returned in a snippety tone, her little nose stuck up in the air. 'You're the one who was hired to do all the thinking!' And with a flip of her skirts she marched out into the living-room and turned on the TV.

Help me control my temper, Valeria Brewster prayed as she watched the stiff back disappear through the doorway. This may be the hardest job I've ever held in my life.

So if it's that difficult, why don't you quit? her conscience nagged at her.

'If I had any sense, I would,' Val murmured. 'The man is impossible and the child is improbable! But——' And there was the rub. Some indefinable something was tugging at her, some force which she could neither describe nor defeat. And it was binding her to this odd couple who needed each other—but obviously didn't need *her*!

Ten o'clock closed in quickly on her busy fingers. There was always work to be done. If not the school, the students, the protests, the community, then it was her knitting, her family accounts, her schemes—and her plans. Schemes were things she definitely meant to do. Plans were more on the order of dreams—things she *wanted* to do but could not see how. The old wall clock struck off another hour.

There was a moon painting the garden, turning all the varieties of red roses to silver. A dozen fire-flies slashed their little billboards off and on among the bushes. The night had gone quiet, so quiet that a dog howled miles away and could be heard clearly in the little garden. And still Bart Thomas slept.

Valeria stood over him. Full-grown males were an oddity in her parochial existence. And here I have one for my very own, her traitorous mind chuckled. She grinned at the thought. With his eyes open, on his feet, he was every inch the predator; sprawled out on the couch, he was a tame puss indeed. But she couldn't leave him out in the garden for much longer. Despite the heat of summer, in the early dawning an on-shore breeze would appear, and a mist would form. Leave him here in the pearly dew? her mind teased. Never happen!

'Mr Thomas?' She touched his shoulder and tugged gently. He grumbled under his breath and inched away from her. 'Mr Thomas?' More definitive, that. More commanding. And totally ignored. 'Oh, dear,' she muttered.

Somehow she had to get him into the house. The living-room would be far enough. She squeezed an arm under his shoulders and tried to lift. An impossible idea. He grunted, and one eye half opened.

'Wassamatta?'

'I have to get you into the house.' The words rushed out in one burst of fire. He grunted again and the eye closed.

Lord, she thought, it isn't going to work. I know it isn't! What now? While her mind pondered, her fingers were busy. If he were to walk, he needed his shoes. It wasn't the easiest task in the world, but she kept at it. Twice he grumbled and moved a foot; she stopped and held her breath. But eventually it was done.

The belt was another problem. Mainly because it was right in the *middle* of him, and her hands fluttered uncontrollably as she struggled with the buckle. It hardly seemed that such a simple device, seen from a normal distance, could be so damnably complicated. Perseverance won, but when she was finished she had to step back to calm her nerves and settle her breathing. Old maid, her conscience nagged at her. Can't stand being that close to a real man! Valeria wiped the perspiration off her brow and wished she wasn't so sensitive.

'Mr Thomas?' A real shake this time instead of a gentle tug at his shoulder. 'Mr Thomas!' Eighth-grade boys had been known to quail at that tone, and Bart Thomas was no exception. He stirred briefly, groaned, and opened one eye.

'The hotel's on fire and we have to escape by the back door,' she rattled on. 'Fire!' Maybe I should have said pirates, she thought as he rumbled and grumbled and came to a sitting position.

'Lean on me,' she prodded. 'The smoke's filling the corridor. Hurry!' With a little assistance he came to his feet and leaned. It had all the effect of Hercules leaning on a matchstick. 'Oh, my,' she muttered as she sagged under his weight. They hobbled across the flagstone path and up the one stair that led into the kitchen.

The kitchen door was in one of its recalcitrant moods. It refused to budge. Valeria managed a half-dozen short round expletives. Bart Thomas opened an eye and tch-tch'd. 'Ladies don't talk like that,' he mumbled.

'Well, I'm no lady,' she snapped back at him as she butted against the door with her ample hip. It surrendered, swinging inward with a squeak of protest. They staggered across the kitchen and into the living-room. It was about as far as Valeria could manage. With a very gusty sigh of relief she guided him to the sofa and watched as he collapsed on it. He was fast asleep again before she could swing his feet up and unlace his shoes.

'I'm glad to see you're comfortable,' she commented softly as she leaned over him. A lock of his hair had fallen forward over his face. With a gentle finger she traced it back where it belonged. The temptation was too great. He was indeed a *great deal* of man. Her lips gently caressed the tanned forehead. After all, there was no way *he* could know. But as she pulled away from the contact, pleased at her deception, one of those dark eyes was open.

Valeria blushed. 'I was——' she stammered, and then stopped talking. A tiny little smile played at the corners of his mouth, and then the eye closed again.

'Playing with fire?' he muttered, and was gone again. Valeria Brewster took a deep breath and climbed the stairs to the bathroom.

'What in the world is the *matter* with me?' she muttered as she faced herself in the mirror. 'I look a mess.' But it was neither face nor figure that worried her as she finished her ablutions and went off to bed. It was her mind. Somehow, secretly, Bart Thomas had pierced the wall of isolation behind which she had hidden since Gran's death. It left her with an uneasy feeling—something she had no wish for at all! Maybe it's all a bad dream, she thought as she finally dropped off to sleep. I'll wake up in the morning and he and his crazy daughter will be gone. I'll have breakfast and a good laugh, and go off to school as usual, and——

Birdsong is beautiful wake-up music. The little flock of finches had haunted her garden all summer, doing their cheerful thing at the bird-feeder. Bart Thomas woke gradually, in sections. The last thing he remembered was a glass of wine. Elderberry wine, for crying out loud! If anyone heard about *this*, he'd be the laughing-stock of Boston. Elderberry wine and a prim little school-teacher who wasn't all that prim in a bathing-suit. Not at all. He wiggled his toes. Everything seemed to be attached and in working order. Now all I have to do, he thought, is get up and walk! He struggled. His head ached slightly from the movement, but the moment he came to a stop everything readjusted itself.

Sunlight was streaming in from the windows. Strange glass. Each pane was composed of a half-dozen smaller circles. Bottle glass—that was what they called it. And a small room with a low ceiling. If he stood up he would have to watch his head. Especially when going through the doorways! He tried gingerly, finding the world not as bad as he had anticipated. The fireplace attracted him.

It was a massive stone structure feeding into a brick chimney. And on the other side, in the kitchen, he reasoned, would be another fireplace sharing the same chimney. But where in the world was the bathroom? A gurgling of pipes gave him a hint. He made his way carefully up the stairs and into the enlarged cupboard that housed all the necessities.

Downstairs in the kitchen, standing at the cooker, working on pancakes, Valeria heard him fumble around, downstairs and up, offered a short prayer that he didn't break his neck. It would be a shame, after all the trouble they had gone through, to lose him so quickly.

When he poked his way around the corner of the kitchen door, she looked up in surprise. He had managed to rescue his lawyer-image. His tie was a little askew, his trousers somewhat rumpled, and a little patch of plaster adorned his chin, but all in all the pompous employer was back.

'Cut yourself shaving?' she asked, for want of something better to say.

'Yes.' He fingered his chin. 'I haven't seen a double-edged safety razor in years. Your father's?'

'Grandpa's,' she corrected as she pulled out a chair for him. 'Maybe the blade wasn't too sharp?'

'No maybe about it,' he chuckled. 'The old guy needs a new blade.'

'I don't think so.' Valeria could feel that instant pang. Grandpa had been all the father she had ever known. 'Gramps passed away about ten years ago,' she told him gently. 'The blade might be even older than that.' She shrugged her shoulders and swept her unbound hair back over her shoulders to get it out of the way. 'Pancakes and real Vermont maple syrup for breakfast?'

'Yes. Coffee,' he added. 'Are those sausages?'

*'Linguiça,'* she advised. 'A spicy Portuguese sausage, yes. Want some?'

'Don't mind if I do.' When he laughed, his face re-arranged itself into something much less pompous, much more attractive. Cut that out. Valeria told her wandering mind. I've enough to put up with without getting personally involved. Lust and breakfast don't go well together!

'After the pancakes, I wouldn't mind an egg or two,' he added reflectively. 'Or maybe three. Fried, over-easy? Where's Maria?'

'She hardly seems to get up before noon,' Valeria reported. 'Maybe she's still on Pacific Standard Time?'

'Maybe she needs a little rousting,' he chuckled. He seemed to inhale about half of his cup of coffee in one fell swoop, and bustled out of the kitchen. Valeria was left with the spatula in hand, caught between daydreams and laughter as the swinging door oscillated back and forth behind him.

Moments later there was a shout of laughter—two voices—from upstairs. A thud of feet, as if someone were chasing somebody down the corridor, the slam of the bathroom door, followed by deep masculine laughter in the corridor, and feminine giggles inside the bathroom, which was located directly over the kitchen. And then he was back, a broad grin on his face.

'She'll be right down,' he said. 'She'll have pancakes.'

'But she won't be satisfied with just pancakes,' Valeria protested. 'The girl has an appetite like a—like—oh, damn!'

'She'll have pancakes,' he assured her. 'And remind me, you need to be reimbursed for all this.' He waved one hand grandly around the kitchen. The other was busy at his fork. The rule about not talking while you ate hardly seemed to fit. His mouth was big enough for both!

His daughter came moments later, swathed in a long cotton granny gown that did little to hide her developing figure. And she ate pancakes.

'So now,' he said later as he helped Valeria stack the dishes in the drain. 'You'll pack up and we'll be on our way.'

'I—on our way?' Val stuttered.

'Of course. We're on our way to our new house. I'm told that everything is ready for us.'

'But I—didn't realise this was a live-in job,' she said. 'I'm not——'

'Everything will be entirely proper,' he laughed. 'I have to be careful of my reputation. We have a housekeeper-cook, a handyman, and Harry. More chaperons than you can shake a stick at.'

'Yes, of course,' she muttered rebelliously. 'We must be careful of *your* reputation!'

His mind worked a thousand times faster than hers, she told herself, as she watched that grin spread across his face. 'And yours, too,' he told her. 'But—the governor is making an appointment to the Bench this week, you know. Something I've always wanted. It will be a tremendous loss in income, but the prestige—well, I'd *kill* for it. And I'm on the shortlist. While the governor's council is investigating, a lawyer must be like Caesar's wife, you know.'

Valeria was unable to stop the teasing. 'Which one?' she asked innocently. 'He was married more than once, you know—and one of them was a woman who could be classified as a Frequent Flyer!'

Bart Thomas fold both his arms in front of him and looked down at her for almost a minute, absolutely quiet, a solemn frown on his face. And then he said, 'Git!' Valeria 'got'.

Packing was not a large problem. A girl with a small wardrobe hardly needed more than two suitcases. When he carried them down the stairs for her, and out into the sunlight, she checked the house to unplug all the appliances except the refrigerator, re-filled the bird-bath and the feeding stations in the back yard, and went around the house. When Val made going-away noises at the front door, Rudolph condescended to stir his ancient frame and wandered along behind.

Maria was already ensconced in the front seat of the Mercedes, Bart was holding open the back door, and Mrs Herlihy was standing by her gate across the street. The old dog had trouble climbing up into the car; Bart picked him up gently and set him down on the seat.

'Overnight visitors?' the neighbourhood gossip called. Valeria waved a hand and wished she wasn't there. Bart helped her into the car and went around to the driver's seat.

He was a conservative driver. They seemed to float out of the driveway and back up the pot-holed road. Valeria twisted in her seat to peer out the back window.

'What's the matter?' Bart stopped at the turn into Summer Street and looked back over his shoulder.

'Reputations,' Val muttered. And then, louder, 'Reputations!'

'You mean the little lady at the fence? So what's that mean?'

'That means that she knows you spent the night in my house,' she sighed. 'Mrs Herlihy. She makes money on the side by writing a column for the local paper.'

'Too bad,' he comforted. 'I suppose in a small town like Plymouth that could do you a little damage. What sort of a column does she write?'

'A gossip column,' Val informed him. 'As if I didn't have enough trouble in my life. Dear God!'

'I'm sorry,' he offered as he started the car moving again. 'I guess I'm glad you didn't introduce me to her. That would be just the titbit my political enemies needed.'

'And your judicial appointment would go down the drain?' she asked cautiously.

'Perhaps not,' he mused. 'I have a lot of friends. But still—you know. What a headline *that* would make! "Would-be Judge in Love-Nest"!'

Valeria winced. Love-nest? Good lord, what would Gran have said to that? 'Well, you'd better brace yourself and hope they spell your name right,' she mused. 'Mrs Herlihy has a lot of friends, too—and she was busy writing down the licence-plate number of your car!'

'Don't worry about it,' he returned. 'It's a rented car.' But she could see his face in the rear-view mirror as he concentrated on the road, and he was undoubtedly a worried man!

# CHAPTER THREE

THE DRIVE through the middle of town was as quiet as a funeral procession. Not a word was spoken until they slowed, made a left turn off Sandwich street and rolled up a semicircular drive to his new home.

'Oh, my!' Valeria gasped. The house was one of the solid brick buildings constructed in the 1920s, when labour had been cheap and the best building materials had been available for use. The two storeys of brick were topped off by massive white-painted wooden eaves and roof. A portico in front reached to the roof, supported by slender Corinthian columns. Surrounding the house itself was almost an acre of billiard-table grass, with ash, maple and oak trees scattered here and there. The shrubbery screened the entire building from both sight and sound of the highway.

'I've lived in Plymouth all my life, but I've never *seen* a place like this before.' Val wriggled her way out of the car and stood with hands on hips, contemplating. Maria came around the car and stood at her side, imitating her stance.

'They've got bigger ones in Beverly Hills,' the child grumbled. 'Lots bigger.'

'I'm sure they have,' Valeria returned gently. 'But this is where we are. Isn't it a nice house?'

'I suppose so. I don't like it, you understand—but I suppose it's not bad.'

'Well, thank you for your understanding,' her father said gruffly. He's still not in good condition, Valeria thought. A headache, maybe. But how could you get a

44

hangover from just a few glasses of Gran's elderberry wine? Distract them both before we have a war!

'Help Rudy out of the car, please.' They all turned to look. The back door was open, and the old dog was poised on the edge, not sure that he wanted to jump.

'Poor old boy,' Maria said sympathetically. She stepped back, hoisted the dog up in her arms, and staggered back to the group. Look at her face, Valeria cautioned herself. Madonna-like. That girl has a lot of affection to give, and the one who receives it will be surely blessed!

She grabbed at Maria's elbow and tugged. 'Why don't we go in?' she prattled, and towed the girl behind her as she mounted the two stairs that led to the front porch. The door opened grandly. A hugely tall, thin woman, white-haired but with eyes full of spirit, introduced herself.

'Mabel Baines,' she said. Maria sniffed. Valeria held out her hand as the child squeezed by them and set the dog down on the tessellated floor.

'Mrs Baines is our housekeeper and cook. She's been with my family for years.' Bart Thomas made the introductions as he came up behind them with Valeria's suitcases. The housekeeper smiled at him and moved to one side. Behind her, completely hidden, was a sharp-faced, thin man no bigger than five feet tall. He moved up to take the suitcases. 'And this is Harry. He's our Lord High Everything Else.' Harry nodded, seized the load, and was gone before Valeria could think of a single thing to say.

'All the work's done,' Mrs Baines assured him. 'But there seems to be a furniture shortage.'

'Oh?' He's not too worried about the problem, whatever it is, Val thought as she studied them both. They seemed to know each other well.

'Everything's complete downstairs, but upstairs—there's only furniture in three bedrooms,' Mrs Baines hurried on. 'The other two bedrooms are empty. Would you like some breakfast?'

'No, Miss Brewster fed us breakfast in great style. I'll call somebody up about the furniture,' he promised as he gestured for Valeria to precede him into the house. 'And in the meantime we only need three. One for Maria, one for Miss Brewster, and the other for myself.'

Mrs Baines still seemed to be on edge, but she relaxed her formal face and gave Valeria a warm smile. That's the answer, Val told herself. Feed my boy, right!

Bart stalked down the hall, looking into each room as he passed, and because he had a giant's grip on Valeria's left hand she went along behind. By the time Mrs Baines caught up with them they had arrived at the room at the back of the house.

'They call it the sun-room,' he announced. No explanation was needed. The walls facing eastward were all french windows, stretching from the parquet floor almost to the ceiling, and looking out toward the ocean. The lawns swept down to within a stone's throw of the waterline, where a stone dock projected out into the shallow bay. Half-way between the house and the bay was a huge fresh-water swimming pool surrounded by a white concrete apron. A figure stirred in the distance, a speck of gold bikini covering a voluptuous figure, but the face was hidden under a wide-brimmed hat.

'Er—one of the bedrooms with the furniture in it has already been claimed,' Mrs Baines stammered. 'Miss Amelé arrived late last night, and——'

'Oh, brother,' Bart groaned. 'I thought she was going to stay in Boston. I take it you found it a little hard to evict her?'

'Just so,' Mrs Baines snorted, her dignity ruffled. 'That woman is——'

'Not good for me,' he laughed. 'I know, Mabel. You've told me often enough. Valeria, you'll have to get used to all this. Mabel was my substitute mother from when I was——'

'Six months old,' Mrs Baines interjected. 'He was always a handful, that one.'

'And I'm sure she'll tell you all about it at the drop of a handkerchief.' He gave the housekeeper a loving hug and received a muttered 'Go on with you' for his troubles.

And why am I so uneasy about all this? Valeria asked herself as a troubled frown formed on her face. So he's got his lady-bird in residence whether he likes it or not, and I can't help but believe he'll like it. If Mabel thinks he was a handful when he was a child, lord, what he must be now?

She snapped back to attention just in time to hear him say, 'Now, if I've got to see about furniture, I'd better get at it. Miss Brewster can go down to the pool and welcome our guest while I make the calls, Mabel.'

'But——' she started to say. He was already gone, cruising down the long, polished hall like one of the ships of the great white fleet, looking for pirates to annihilate.

'But I'm only an employee,' she muttered under her breath. 'I didn't come here to be your hostess. And she probably knows you a great deal better than I do.'

Mabel Baines, who had exceptionally good hearing for a woman her age, wiped her hands on her apron before patting Valeria on the shoulder. 'A great deal better,' she said solemnly, and then broke out laughing. 'I like you, Valeria Brewster,' she said. 'He's a very imperious sort of man. Your dog is asleep under the stove in my kitchen. Is that all right?'

'He's very old,' Val explained. 'He's really my grand-mother's dog. If he won't disturb you there, I suspect that's the best place for him. He doesn't go out very much these days.'

'It's no trouble,' the housekeeper answered, and she too spun on her heel and went loping off down the hall.

Valeria walked slowly over to the nearest french window and stopped, one hand on the latch, the other fingering the beautiful transparent curtains. 'So why should *I* be the sacrificial goat?' she muttered. 'I don't know a single thing about the woman except that I don't like her. I wonder if she could be Dr Fell's daughter?' The idea recalled the ancient little poem. She chanted it as she straightened her shoulders, tugged at her simple skirt, and turned the knob.

The grass was trimmed neatly, but thick underfoot. Walking across it was like taking a stroll on a waterbed. And the closer she got to the pool, the less she liked the whole idea.

Amelé Poitras had heard her coming, and was sitting up on a lounge chair, hat in hand, watching. The gold bikini was gradually losing the war against modesty. Tanned flesh protruded in all sorts of curves and corners. If she's not careful she's going to fall out of it, Val assured herself. But it's all wasted on me.

'It's about time somebody came,' the blonde grumbled. 'What took you so long?'

'I don't think I know what you're talking about,' Val returned primly.

'I rang more than fifteen minutes ago,' Amelé insisted. 'I want something cool to drink. A Piña Colada.'

'Yes, I bet that *would* be tasty.' Valeria smoothed her skirt underneath her and settled into a more solid single chair. 'I had one once, three or four years ago,' she said dreamily. 'Very tasty.'

'I don't want to spend a lot of time listening to your reminiscences,' the other girl said sharply. 'Go and get me my drink.'

Valeria stared at the woman. In the strong sunlight she had hoped to see black roots in Amelé's blonde hair, but to no avail. The woman was perfection. Damn! But anger twisted Amelé's face into an ugly mask and seemed to add fifteen years to her age. Grandpa's wry voice ran through Val's mind. 'But put a brown paper bag over her head and she'd look a stunner,' the old man would say. So right. But I'm here to maintain the peace!

'Perhaps if you rang again, Harry might come,' she suggested. 'He's been busy moving our luggage around. I imagine bringing drinks falls into his line of work. I'd be happy to help you, but I haven't the vaguest idea where anything is.'

Ice dripped from Amelé's voice, 'One of the things I hate most is impertinent servants.'

So now the rules of the game are being defined. Val thought. She wants to play hard-ball. 'I feel the same way,' she returned artlessly. 'Of course, I can't remember ever having an impertinent servant. Come to think of it, I can't remember ever having a servant!'

'Well, I——' Amelé screamed, half rising from her lounger.

'You shouldn't do that,' Val interrupted coolly. 'It gives you wrinkles and you come all-over with the uglies. And for your information, Miss Poitras, I'm not a servant.'

Amelé fell back into her chair, gasping for breath, her cool, tanned face turning a mottled red.

One more turn of the screw, Valeria thought. 'I'm a schoolteacher, Miss Poitras. What do *you* do for a living?' Val cut the question short. Besides sleeping around, she had wanted to add.

'Do?' Amelé queried. 'Why should I *do* anything? I don't have to grub around to make a living. My father provides for me adequately. He's a State senator, you know!'

Valeria, to whom the information was a total surprise, took a deep breath before continuing the attack, but the sight of Maria and Bart coming down the hill, hand in hand, dressed in swimwear, was reason enough to cut the discussion short. Peace-keeping is a difficult business! she told herself, and clenched her teeth to stop the flow of words.

Amelé saw them at the same moment, and performed one of those magical changes only possible to the 'wicked witch' class of females. She mastered her anger, made some minimum adjustments to her bikini and hair, and became the cool, blonde lovely.

'Maria, my dear,' she gushed. 'How good to see you. You look well this morning.' It was true. In her form-fitting suit the girl had a voloptuous figure, and could easily be taken for someone twice her age.

'Ha!' the girl snorted as she turned her back on the assembly and walked around to the other side of the pool.

'Maria!' her father called harshly. The child stared at them insolently, then plunged into the water. 'I can't do a thing with that girl,' he muttered to Valeria. 'That's what I want you to do—bring her to some sort of order!'

'It all begins with love,' Valeria cautioned him. 'You must realise that the primary thought of every child of divorced parents is that her father and mother still love each other and want to get back together.'

'Fat chance,' he snapped. 'Eleanore is getting re-married in a week. To some dumb film producer. The child is just going to have to learn.'

'It seems to me,' Amelé contributed, 'that the only solution is for you to remarry, Bart. That will snap the little monster out of her spell.'

'She's *not* a little monster,' Valeria chided. 'She's just a misunderstood and misunderstanding child. With a little practice, I'm sure she could turn sweet.'

Two disbelieving faces turned at her. 'Come on in, Dad,' Maria called as she whipped across the pool in a very credible backstroke. 'It's cold, but it's nice!'

'Yes, well——' Bart hesitated, looked at each of the women as if he had never seen them before. 'Come join us,' he offered Amelé. 'There's no sense in letting that neat bathing-suit go to waste.'

'She can't swim in that thing,' his daughter called. The girl was hanging on the edge of the pool's concrete apron, just at their feet. 'That's one of those *looking-at* suits, not a *swimming-in* suit!'

'I really shouldn't,' Amelé protested. 'My hair—and I ought to run up to the house. I have something I must do.' She stretched up on tiptoes and kissed Bart's cheek.

'Then I'll come with you,' he insisted. The pair of them walked up the slope toward the house, holding hands. Once again that little tingle of—regret?—ran through Valeria's mind. He was such a fine figure of a man, running from broad square shoulders to narrow waist, his muscles firm under the tanned skin. Narrow hips too, supported by strong thighs and long legs. His miniscule trunks were almost the same colour as his tanned skin, so that in the distance he looked nude.

'Hey!' A cold hand touched Valeria's arm and brought her down to earth. Maria was dripping at her side. 'You could come in the pool,' the girl said condescendingly.

'I don't have my swimsuit on.'

'You could get it.'

'You weren't all this friendly earlier today.' Val grinned down at the serious face, hardly an inch or two below her own. You're going to be a big girl, Maria, she thought. A big, good-looking girl. We'll get that hair to grow out, and clean it up considerably, and cut down on some of that chubby baby-fat, and—good lord, what a long-term project that all will be. And I won't be around that long! If there were a tinge of regret in her thought, she could hardly explain where it came from.

'Well, everything considered,' Maria answered thoughtfully, 'you're not really too bad to have around. Compared to somebody like that Amelé, I mean, only——'

'How kind of you to say so,' Valeria interrupted, laughing.

'I mean—well, you're not too bad as a companion,' Maria continued stubbornly, 'but you hafta get that "stupid cow" look off your face. My dad and my mom are gonna get back together any day now, and you hafta——'

'*Hafta* keep my claws off him?'

The girl winced. 'Have to,' she said. 'Yes, you have to keep your claws off my dad. Or else——'

'Or else the sky will fall, Chicken Little,' Val teased. 'I'll go get my swimsuit, and we'll see who's queen of the pool.' She rested a cool hand on the child's shoulder for a moment, and then walked slowly up to the house. And the girl means every word of it, Val thought as she walked. She means to do damage to any woman who dares to fall in love with her father. But since I don't plan any such stupidity, maybe we can get along. Add Maria to Mrs Baines, on my side. Harry? I just don't know. Amelé Poitras? If I were flat-chested and buck-toothed, little Amelé would still hate me. That leaves only Mr Thomas. Mr Bartholomew Thomas, Esquire. Lord, is he ever an enigma!

He was the sort of enigma you would not want to run into at sea in a small boat. 'In here,' he said harshly as she came up the corridor. And one of his big hands assisted in the movement. The other slammed the door behind him.

'Now, I won't put up with *that*!' His voice was threateningly soft, and his eyes brooded at her.

Caught unawares, she stuttered for a moment. 'No, I wouldn't either. Put up with what?'

'Amelé was practically in tears from the savaging you gave her. I didn't hire you to aggravate my—er—guests, and I don't intend to see it happen again. When Amelé desperately needs help, I expect you to give it willingly. Is that clear?'

'Needs help desperately?' Valeria shook her head to clear her ears. Her long wine-red hair fell down and swirled around her head. 'A Piña Colada is a desperate need?'

'She said you'd say something like that,' he continued humourlessly. 'She seems to know your sort of woman like a book. And it's got to stop!'

'I see,' she returned coldly. 'You believe every word she says, and there's a big 'if' in your statement. And if it doesn't stop, then what?'

'Then I'll have to dispense with your services,' he said ponderously.

Valeria could feel the anger welling up, choking her throat. She stood for a moment, feet slightly apart, hands at her sides but clenched until the fingernails bit into her palms. 'Well then, Mr Thomas,' she stated flatly. 'Do please let me save you some time and trouble. I quit right now!'

'Oh, no, you don't,' he muttered. She turned away, trying to reach the door. One of his hands clapped on to her shoulder and whirled her around. She staggered from the thrust. His other arm came up to support her, and before she knew it, she was wrapped up in his arms, her breasts bruising his bare upper torso. Struggle as she might, she could not free either of her arms. And he was bending over her, coming close enough to block out the light.

'No—I——' But there was no time for words. His lips came down on hers, soft and moist and warm, and sealed off the conversation.

Valeria prided herself in being up to date. She had kissed her share of boys in her day, although not lately, and she knew that all she had to do was to stand still and quiet and make no response. Unfortunately, she had never been kissed with such expertise before. The standing still was nothing; the making no response was impossible. There was fire running up and down her spine, and when he relaxed his grip so that she could move her arms, they went unbidden up and around his neck.

She stood on tiptoes for a moment, and when she relaxed he lifted her up off her feet entirely, without disengaging. Rage was succeeded by passion, and then passion by panic. One of her flailing feet managed to contact his ankle. The shock brought him back to his senses, and he lowered her gently to the floor.

His arms were still around the small of her back. She leaned against his strength to focus on his face. 'I didn't mean to do that,' he drawled. 'But it was pleasant. I suppose you want to slap my face?'

'You're darned right,' she sighed. 'Later, when I get my strength back.'

'Funny, that,' he agreed. 'I never ever thought of kissing as a physical exercise, but it *does* take a lot out of you, doesn't it?'

It's all a game with him, Valeria told herself. All a great big joke. And if I let him get away with it, he'll think he's got one of those women who can't say no. Now's the time to do something drastic! She had managed by this time to free both arms. One of his hands was wandering over the contours of her face, and he made a tactical mistake.

Her sharp white teeth bit into his finger with all the emphasis Valeria could muster. He made a little squeak of pain, and then roared as the sharp point of her shoe bounced off his shin.

'Dear God,' he rumbled, taking a step or two away from her. 'What was *that* all about?'

'I don't like it when men make unsolicited use of my body,' she said very primly. 'Next time, ask first.'

He had his injured finger in his mouth. Now, as he took it out to look for blood, he gave a dry chuckle. 'So there'll be a next time, will there?'

'Not if I can help it,' she muttered. 'You owe me three days' pay. Please mail it to me!'

'I said you weren't going to quit,' he roared back at her. She let it all go right over her head. Grandpa Brewster had been a roarer, so she knew all about that sort of man. Valeria started toward the door and bumped into Harry as she set foot in the corridor.

'Come back here,' Bart Thomas yelled angrily.

'I'm about to do you a big favour,' she shouted at him.

'Favour?' He went suddenly quiet, as if someone had just given him an unwanted injection of caution.

'Favour,' she insisted. 'I'm going home. Now you won't have to go to all that trouble to get yourself another set of bedroom furniture!'

'But I've——' he started to say.

'I need to go back into town,' she told Harry, interrupting whatever it was that Bart had started to say. 'Is there some way you could call me a taxi?'

'You're a taxi,' the little man said solemnly.

'Dear lord, I don't mean *call* me one like that—I mean get on the telephone and—oh, what the heck, you're all a bunch of nuts! I'll walk.'

Mabel was standing at the front door, holding it open. Rudolph, disgruntled at having his sleep disturbed, stood by the door, panting. Valeria strode up to them, still angry, and dared the housekeeper to add a word. She did.

'I quit sixteen times in the first ten days I worked for the family,' the gaunt, elderly woman said. 'I'll send your luggage after you?'

'Please.' Valeria's lips twitched as she fought to maintain a solemn face. Until that moment she hadn't realised how silly they all were acting. But *she* had no intention of being the first to reform.

'No use walkin' when I've got a perfectly good car standin' doin' nothin',' Harry quipped as he walked through the door behind her, jiggling a set of car keys.

'Don't any of you people *dare* to help that—that woman,' Bart Thomas called as he hurried along at the rear of the procession. 'You can't quit, Valeria Brewster!'

'Don't forget to mail me my cheque,' she yelled back at him, leaning out the window of the Mercedes. And then she leaned back against the soft cushions, folded her arms across her breasts, and hung on for dear life as her body trembled and shook in the reaction that always followed her bursts of anger.

They were passing through the town square, under the eyes of the court and the old Pilgrim burial site atop Burial Hill when Harry made a remark about not knowing where her house was located. That comment, in his Brooklyn accent, broke the ice.

'And he's really one hell of a guy,' Harry said as he coasted up to the kerb beside her house. 'All the stuff he's done for me and mine. And he wasn't always wealthy, you know. Started out without a pit to hiss in, he did. Earned his way through law school. We thought he was gonna be happy with that Mrs Thomas—but she turned out to be as woolly-headed as you could ask. Just *had* to be an actress, and all that garbage. He's lucky without her.'

'But is Maria?' she asked, unwilling to leave the car until she posed that one important question.

'She ain't now,' Harry replied. 'But she will be. Or— she would have been, if you—well, you know how those things are.' He killed the engine and came around to open the car door for her. It was a little gesture out of the past, but it made a wonderful impression.

'Thank you, Harry.' She held out her hand, to find his surprisingly strong and sure. 'I hope we'll see each other again some time.'

'Oh, we will,' he laughed. 'The boss gets riled, but he knows which side of the bread the butter's on. He'll be around, Miss Brewster.'

'Valeria,' she prompted. He grinned a grin as wide as the Grand Canyon.

'Miss Valeria,' he compromised, and touched a finger to his cap in salute before he climbed back in and drove off. Valeria watched the car disappear before she turned towards home. Across the street the curtains moved in the front window. Subconsciously she noticed that too, but paid it no attention.

She was fumbling with the keys to her front door when she heard the sound. 'Hoo-hoo—Valeria!' She turned around and shook her head. Mrs Herlihy was descending on her with notebook in hand. Rudolph growled. Old as he was, he could still distinguish friend from foe. 'Hush, Rudy,' Val admonished.

'You know I was always such a close friend of your grandmother,' the newspaper woman babbled. It wasn't so. Val thought. In fact, Grandmother had more than once held Mrs Herlihy up to me as the model of what becomes of a girl who doesn't study hard and eat her vegetables.

'Just who was that charming gentleman I saw come out of the house with you this morning, Valeria? ' The pencil was poised, waiting. Mrs Herlihy had a number of troublesome habits, but the one that annoyed Valeria the most was that the woman's nose continually dripped, the result of some allergy probably. It was not something that the woman could help, but Val had closed her heart against this snooper. It dripped now.

'I don't think I can tell you that,' Val said primly. 'The gentleman employed me to do some—er—tutorial work with his daughter. I don't think he would want his name known.'

'Tutorial work? Staying all night?' The newshound's nose twitched almost as fast as her pencil wrote.

'I think you must have been deceived,' Val maintained stoutly. 'He came early, and stayed while his daughter packed. Good day, Mrs Herlihy. Give your husband my regards.' With that she turned her back and went into the house, not even watching for the look of fury that would automatically follow. Mr Herlihy, after ten years of a nagging marriage, had gone out to buy some cigarettes in the spring of 1972, and hadn't been seen since.

The house had that closed-up feeling; stale air hung heavily in the small rooms. She went around opening windows as her first endeavour, and then, recognising her lack of lunch, strolled into the kitchen to see what might be edible.

'Not much,' she muttered as she constructed a grilled cheese sandwich for herself and a dish of dogfood for Rudy. 'Something will have to be done about my food.' And a glance down her tiny frame. 'And something will have to be done about my wardrobe!' And then, as she collapsed into one of the sturdy wooden chairs in the kitchen, 'And something's got to be done about my love-life! If any.'

She took the sandwich, her dog and her worries out into the back yard with her, stretching out on the lounger in the shade of the old maple tree. Every time she closed her eyes she saw Bart Thomas wandering around on the inside of her eyelids. Smiling, laughing, taunting Bart Thomas.

There's no reason why he should make that much of an impression on you, her very sensible conscience argued. You've only known him for a day or two. To be honest, for a couple of hours! What's the matter?

'Shut up,' Valeria grumbled. Bart Thomas, haunting her, was now kissing Amelé Poitras. Not only that, but he acted as if he were enjoying it! With a snarl of frustration Valeria sent her paper plate winging across the garden, spilling what was left of her sandwich on the grass. Two golden finches zoomed down on to the free lunch, and were instantly driven off by a ragged old magpie.

'Shoo!' she yelled at the bunch of them as she went dragging her feet back into the house. The nerve of that Bart Thomas, she raged to herself. Not only is he a troublemaker in his own place, but he has the colossal gall to come and haunt *my* house!

She found her way back into the living-room, turned on the fan, and slouched down in the old sofa with her feet up. Since she didn't *intend* to sleep, Morpheus came and conquered. The church bells were ringing the Angelus when she woke up.

The little rocking chair that stood opposite the sofa was swinging and creaking. It had been *her* childhood chair, and her mother's before her. And now, in the soft light of the late afternoon, it held Maria Thomas.

The girl was almost as dishevelled as she had been on that first day, with the single exception that her hair was not dyed. She hunched forward in the chair, one foot flat on the floor, rocking, and stared at Valeria intently.

'When you wake up, I need to talk to you,' the girl said.

Valeria stretched. 'Yes, as soon as I wake up I'll remember that. Run away from home, did you?'

'Yes. And I'm *never* going back?'

'Of course not. Who would?' Valeria had trouble hiding the smile. This was the procedure she had used a dozen or more times on students who thought they were too tough for the school system. It always left them gasping, as now.

'You mean—you don't think I ought to go back?'

'I mean it's not up to me to make up your mind for you,' she returned gently. 'If for some reason you think home is not the place for you, then it's your decision to make, not mine. Of course, that leaves you with finding a roof over your head, and a place where you can eat. Unless you brought a great deal of money with you?'

'No, I—didn't think about that.' Maria's chubby chin was quivering. Well after all, thirteen's not exactly a lot of years, Val thought. There was an appeal in the girl's eyes, but it had to be expressed in words, she knew. So she sat quietly on the sofa and waited.

It came at last, in a high, strained voice that reflected Maria's worries. 'But—aren't you going to help me?'

'Ah. Help you?' Valeria stood up and stretched. 'What exactly is it that you think I can help you with?'

'I thought—you wouldn't mind if I lived here for a while.' The words tumbled out in a rush.

'I don't mind,' Val answered. 'Of course, I have a few ground rules, like cleanliness and stuff like that. But the thing that worries me is that your father is bound to come here looking for you. Then what?'

'I could hide and you could tell him you've never seen me.' Maria had wishes glistening in her eyes. Or maybe it was tears and fear. Valeria hesitated, and then committed herself.

'I couldn't lie about it,' she said firmly. 'I don't lie about anything important, not for anybody.' Maria's face fell. It definitely was tears. 'But I know a thing or two about men that you don't,' Val continued. 'You're going about this all wrong, you know.'

'What do you mean?'

'I think you have to recognise that men aren't like us real people,' Val mused.

'Oh, I know that!' the child interrupted.

'No, you don't,' Val chuckled. 'I don't mean the outward stuff that you can *see*. Men don't even *think* the way we do. And they grow up with the idea that since they're bigger than we are, they must be right.'

'I couldn't put up with *that* kind of thinking,' Maria said bitterly.

'Neither could I. And I don't,' Valeria replied. 'But take your dad, for example. Could you out-wrestle him?'

'Of course not! He's way too big for me.' Maria got up from her chair for the first time and went over to the front windows.

'Well, if you can't out-wrestle him you have to out-think him,' Val continued. 'For example, what's your biggest problem right now?'

'That Amelé Poitras,' Maria snapped. 'She's a fake. She plays around my dad so obviously, you'd think he'd know she's making a fool out of him. I think she wants to marry him, and my mother wouldn't stand for that!'

'But I thought your mother was getting married to some movie director?' Valeria called up all her senses, waiting for this answer. It was the key to that complex person called Maria Thomas.

'That's a lie,' Maria answered sharply. 'She wouldn't do a thing like that. It's a lie. Somebody made it up just to—just to——' And the tears rolled like Mississippi waters.

Valeria moved over and put her arms around the weeping child. The sobbing gradually diminished, the trembling came to a halt. Still Val hugged her close. When finally the streaked face lifted the inch or two needed to put them at eyeball level, Valeria fetched her handkerchief and dried those deep-ringed eyes.

'Now,' she said in as practical a tone as she could muster, 'you go take a quick bath, and after that I'm going to tell you how to get along with your father.'

The girl gave her one extra hug for effort, and then stepped away and looked out the window. 'I guess you'd better talk fast,' she said. 'I think that's him now.'

# CHAPTER FOUR

VALERIA was busy at the desk in the library of the Thomas home three days later, sketching out another in the series of appeals against the re-opening of Pilgrim 1, the nuclear power plant just south of town. Night shadows had long since eclipsed the view of the harbour. She chewed on the top of her ballpoint drawing-pen. After six months of pamphleteering, it was difficult to come up with a new idea. When Bart strolled in through the open door she shuffled the papers underneath a brown paper envelope and offered him a weak sort of smile.

'Here's where you're hiding,' he commented as he came in. 'Did you get all your things moved?' She nodded, speechless. 'I certainly didn't mean you to have to share a room with Maria for two nights,' he continued. 'I didn't realise that getting furniture in was all that difficult.'

'I didn't mind at all,' Val said. 'Although your daughter has a slight sleeping problem.'

'She snores,' he chuckled. 'Well, I *did* offer to let you share *my* room.' Valeria made a little face at him.

'Or Amelé's,' he added. Val shuddered.

'You and Amelé don't get along together, do you?' It was a question that hardly needed an answer. Val sniffed disdainfully. 'And Maria doesn't get along well with her, either. And that brings up another question that I don't understand,' he continued, yawning. 'Maria has—well, almost changed her skin.'

63

'Too good to be true?' Valeria, who had been privy to the thoughts of both sides for the last three days, proceeded with some caution. Her little predictions to both Bart and his daughter were almost self-fulfilling. And I'm not sure that the common law against witchcraft has been rescinded in the Commonwealth, she thought wryly.

'Exactly. Too good to be true. She runs away from home, I catch up with you both, ready to apologise for all my sins and the world's, and instead *she* apologises to me——'

'And you kiss and make up,' Val laughed. 'I like that sort of ending.'

'A true romantic at heart, aren't you?' he commented as he sank into one of the upholstered chairs facing the fireplace.

'Your apology was very—nice,' she hazarded. 'Most expressive. You almost made *me* feel guilty.'

'As to the manor born?' He reached for his pipe as he looked around the almost bare room. 'I wasn't, you know. We've got to do something about this room, Valeria.'

The caressing sound of her name gave her a little shiver. He had a marvellous courtroom voice, deep and resonant, and capable of sending sparks up the spine of any woman, eight to eighty!

'All it needs is books,' she commented. 'Shelves, and books. I could buy you some fakes if you want.'

The pipe refused to start. He knocked ash from it into the floor-standing ashtray, and tried again. 'Fake books or fake shelves?'

'You know—rows of make-believe books. Ends with names printed on them, but nothing inside. Most impressive. Tell me about how you came to be a lawyer.'

'Not with fake books,' he chuckled. 'And there really isn't much to tell. My father—well, let's just say he had some bad experiences with the law and its judges. So I managed to get a football scholarship, and half a dozen part-time jobs, and eventually I passed the bar exam.'

'Well, I'm sure there's more than that,' she sighed. 'You're a self-made man. That means a lot these days.'

'There's an old joke about that,' he mused. 'I hope you didn't have *it* in mind.'

'How does it go?' She was only half-paying attention to the words. It was the looks, the attitudes that held her. He was dressed in his usual casual dress. A grey suit, white shirt, jacket and waistcoat. What made it casual was that he had loosened his tie. What he needs is six pairs of jeans and a bonfire for those darn suits, she told herself.

'It goes like this,' he said. 'The English claim to be a self-made people, thus relieving God of a terrible responsibility.'

'Oh! I—didn't mean anything derogatory about you,' she stammered. 'I think a self-made man is the—oh, I don't know what I mean. Tell me some more about your law-life. You became a corporate lawyer right away?'

'No, of course not.' He grimaced, and for a moment puffed on his pipe. The sweet odour drifted over to her. Normally she hated to have people smoke near her, but for some reason she approved of *him* doing so.

'No,' he continued. 'When I came out of law school I was filled with the spirit of moralistic crusade, and set to reform the world. I went into the public defenders' office in New York City. You know the bit, I'm sure. You take on all the sure losers, for practically no pay.' His pipe was drawing smoothly now. He took a slow draught, and then blew out a perfectly circular ring of smoke. She stared at it, entranced, as it rose toward the ceiling. 'But I met Eleanore at the same time. Lord, she was lovely in those days!'

The thought seemed to hold him in a dream for a moment.

'And you fell in love at first sight?' Valeria prodded at him, wanting—no, needing—to hear more. Her long hair was tight on her head. She pulled at a couple of pins and let it cascade down around her head.

Bart Thomas seemed to come to some decision. 'Yeah. Love and marriage and Maria, all at once. But Eleanore wanted to be an actress, and I wasn't making enough money, so finally she split. One year to the day after our wedding, she ran out for the West Coast. I thought it might happen, but I didn't expect her to take the baby with her.' He looked at the end of his pipe as if the tobacco had suddenly turned bitter, and then knocked the dottle out into the ashtray.

'That must have been a terrible surprise.' It was almost impossible for Valeria to keep the sympathy out of her voice. The warm, tender sympathy which was so much a part of her own personality. 'And then what?'

'And then,' he said, and the bitterness was in his voice now, not in his pipe. 'And then I decided that since money was the way people are judged, I'd go out and make some. So I went into the stock-market in a big way, managed to come out with a bundle, and set up my own corporation in Boston. And you know something——'

'Yes,' Valeria said quietly. 'Once you'd got the money, you found you didn't want to be judged by it, after all!'

He looked over at her, as if seeing her differently in that single second of speech. 'Smart,' he commented. 'You're smarter than——'

'Than I look?'

'Good lord, no. Not that. You *look* smart. That's why I assumed that you *weren't*. Women are like that, you know.'

'Are they really? I didn't know.' He caught the little touch of sarcasm in her naïve answer and barked a sharp little laugh.

'Yes, they are, really,' he assured her. 'Having found my pot of gold, I also found a goodly number of women ready to explain life to me—in a variety of ways. There isn't anything I don't know about women, Valeria Brewster. So don't try any little tricks on me.'

'I wouldn't dare,' she murmured. But her eyes twinkled and the little muscle at the corner of her mouth twitched, a sure indication that Valeria Brewster was up to no good at just that moment.

'Now, about my daughter,' he suggested.

'Maria? She's going through a stage,' Val said gently. 'Girls do that, you know. She's decided that shocking you into compliance didn't work, so now she's going to charm you. You know the bit: you catch more flies with honey than with vinegar.'

'What is it she's shocking me into?'

'Love. Marriage,' Valeria said, ducking her head away from him to hide the little blush of embarrassment.

'Marriage?' He shook his head in disgust. 'That's one trap I won't fall into twice. Who in the world does she want me to marry?'

'Her mother, of course.' Valeria swallowed her laughter as the look of horror spread over Bart's face. He might never have thought that thought until she brought it up—but nothing could be more certain than that he had no intention of complying with his daughter's wishes.

'Re-marry?' he asked, aghast. 'Eleanore and I? That's about as likely as the Republicans electing a governor in Massachusetts. I think I'd rather have Maria rude and restless and dirty, than clean and concerned and pursuing *that* idea!' He shook his head and then got to his feet in a smooth, flowing motion. 'I hope you're not encouraging her along those lines?'

'I don't encourage or discourage,' Val replied. 'As I see it, my business is support, not suppression.'

'Yes, I—your hair is beautiful, Valeria.' It was such a sudden change of direction that for a moment Val had no idea what ought to come next. He stalked over in front of her and toyed with the streaming mass of silky strands. 'Beautiful.' A low-voiced murmur, as if he were caught in the web of it.

She stood patiently, unmoving, not sure of either herself or him. The fingers roamed gently, came down around her cheeks, and touched gently on her patrician nose. 'Altogether beautiful,' he murmured.

It was more than Valeria could handle. A little shudder ran up and down her spine as she backed away from him. Now it was *his* turn to remain fixed in position. His hand was still raised to the level of her face, and a look of—embarrassment—flashed across his face before he recovered.

'Yes. Where were we?'

'Your daughter,' she reminded, pushing her hair back over her shoulders so it would be almost out of sight. She had never known a man with a hair fetish. But it takes all kinds, she told herself. I wish I'd not taken it down! And yet, it hadn't been a terrible thing. His hands, so large when seen at a distance, had been remarkably gentle. And pleasant!

'Yes, my daughter,' he repeated. 'Do you have some suggestions?'

'Only one,' Valeria replied. 'Do things *with* her. Share some of your time and energy. Let her see close-up that you love her as much as—that you love her.'

'As much as her mother does?' he said glumly. 'That wouldn't be hard. I had a private detective investigate them a year ago. Her mother spent all her time on the go, leaving Maria in the hands of maids and baby-sitters——'

'And companions,' Valeria interjected. He had the courtesy to blush.

'And companions,' he sighed, agreeing. 'But none so well qualified as you.'

'I hate to talk myself out of a job,' Val commented, 'but that's really what Maria needs. Your wholehearted attention. I'd think you would want that, too. You said you wanted to be a judge?'

'With a passion. More than anything I know of,' he returned. 'I've made enough money to live on. I can afford to work at the State's salary scale, and it's something I promised my—someone—I would do for him. So?'

Scratch 'someone' and write in 'father.' Val thought. But he doesn't want to admit it. Oh, well. 'Well, judges are appointed for life,' she said, 'but first they need to be confirmed by the governor's council, a purely political body. So what better way to get yourself confirmed than by appearing in public with your daughter? The "family man" routine. It always goes over well in Massachusetts.'

'Maybe I should fire you as a companion and sign you up as my political adviser,' he chuckled.

'I—don't have time for that,' she confessed nervously. 'I'm too much involved in the nuclear power plant thing.'

'I remember.' He came over by the desk and put a finger on top of her papers as she held her breath, but that was the extent of his investigation. 'What can I do to help? We really need that electrical power!'

Sup with the devil, Val thought, and then see if you can steal some of his table utensils? And why not? What

he don't know won't hurt him! But if he finds out, her
conscience nagged, there will be hell to pay! She mentally flipped a coin. It came down on edge and refused
to fall on either side. Val shrugged her shoulders.

'Yes, as it happens, there is something,' she said,
putting on her best air of innocence. 'My old photocopier is falling apart, and I——'

'Say no more,' he laughed, raising his hand as a stop
sign. 'I'll have one brought out tomorrow. Would you
want it right in here?'

'Wonderful.' Her whole face sparkled. Push your luck,
she thought. 'And tomorrow Maria and I are going down
to the State Pier to wander around among the historical
relics. Why don't you come, too?'

They walked along Water Street like a real family. Maria
danced in the middle, using a hop-skip-jump procedure
to keep up with her long-legged father. Valeria was on
the other side, doing her best despite shorter legs and a
constricting skirt. Her hair was tied back in a ponytail,
as was the girl's. It made them look almost of the same
generation, with their father in tow. He made a remark
or two along those lines.

The on-shore breeze of early morning had died. The
sun reigned supreme. Plymouth baked in its own juices.
'But I still don't see,' Maria repeated as they came off
the pier alongside which lay the Mayflower II, the replica
of the original sailing ship which had brought the
Pilgrims to the inhospitable winter shores of New
England. 'They had one hundred and one members of
the company, and twenty-five sailors, all squeezed into
a boat hardly ninety feet long and twenty-five feet wide?
Somebody's padding the account.'

'It's real,' Valeria assured her. 'Of course, that was
the beginning account. There was a death on the way,

and one birth. But they managed to survive for sixty-six days, through storm and strife. Do you wonder they called themselves "Saints"? All for religion.'

'Freedom of religion is an important concept,' Bart commented laughingly.

'Freedom *from* religion, more likely,' Val chuckled. 'The Pilgrims wanted the right to practice their own brand of religion, free from the Anglican Church. And when they got here they made darn sure that no *other* theology took root in their little colony. And now there you have it.' She pointed up ahead of them to where a little stone pavilion, shaped in the manner of a miniature ancient Greek temple, stood at the side of the road, some feet above the water level.

'That's it?' Maria asked glumly. 'That's Plymouth Rock?'

'That's it.' Valeria led the way up to the granite base that supported more than a dozen Corinthian columns. In the middle of the enclosure, surrounded by a further iron fence, was the old rock—or what was left of it. A later hand than the Pilgrims had scribed '1620' on its side.

'Come *on* now,' the girl grumbled. 'The story is that they came to the shore in their small boat, and stepped out of the boat on to the rock and came to land without getting their feet wet. That's impossible. The darn shore line must be fifty feet away! Has the ocean receded that much in three hundred fifty years?'

'Same rock,' Val insisted, laughing. 'But it's been moved a time or two. Back in the eighteen-fifties half of what you see here was an insert in the middle of Town Wharf. Then it was decided to cement the two halves together and re-establish it up here where people could admire.'

'And not take samples home,' Bart interjected. 'Vandalism has a lot to do with its size today. Before the vandals got at it, the Rock was twenty-three feet in diameter. Now it's less than half that. And I——'

'Mr Thomas? Judge Thomas?' All three of them froze in position. Valeria's heart almost dropped through her boots. The journalist, Mrs Herlihy, had finally caught up. The reporter was showing enough teeth to be rated a tiger shark. 'The governor has just announced your nomination to the Bench, Judge Thomas. What's your reaction?'

'Oh, hell,' he muttered. 'Reporters? Not now!'

'Our readers will be interested,' the woman coaxed.

Valeria struggled with a cough. It was either that or laugh, and he would never forgive laughter. Maria could sense something going on, but could not reason it out. She stood at her father's side, shifting her weight from one foot to the other impatiently.

'Politics,' Val hissed. Out of the corner of her eye she could see him nod, and a plastic grin covered his face.

'Nominated already?' Valeria watched his charisma spark and glow and grow, until it engulfed Mrs Herlihy. 'I had heard rumours, of course. I'm—delighted to serve the Commonwealth in any way I can.'

But Martha Herlihy, on the far side of fifty, was no mean reporter. 'It's very unusual for a divorced man to be given such a nomination,' she pried. 'What do you think of that?'

'Is that a question?' he quipped. 'Divorces do happen, even to prospective judges. By the way, this is my daughter, Maria.'

The girl gave an impertinent shrug of her shoulders and turned her back on them all to stare out to sea. 'She's come to live with me,' he added. 'Permanently.'

'How nice for you,' Mrs Herlihy gushed, and then threw another stiletto. 'Her mother is an actress? One hears that she has performed in some minor parts in some—er—rated pictures.'

Maria whirled around and glared at them. 'My mother is the world's best actress,' she snapped. 'And I'm only here temporarily. My mother and father are——'

'Maria!' It was a gentle caution, emphasised by one of his hands on her shoulder, but it turned her off. She looked up at her father with a tear in each eye, and turned blindly away.

'Maria hasn't settled in yet,' he continued urbanely. 'We're setting up a home here in Plymouth.'

'Yes, I know.' Mrs Herlihy was busy with her second pencil. 'I went to the house, and a lovely lady explained to me where you could be found today. Wasn't that nice of her?'

'Lovely.' Hoping to relieve some of the pressure, Valeria intervened. 'I suppose that was Miss Poitras, the daughter of Senator Poitras?'

'Ah—I suppose.' Mrs Herlihy had not known *who* the woman was. All she knew was that as the front door opened to her knock, someone had told Miss Poitras that Bart was out with his daughter and Valeria. That bit of information had brought on fireworks of monumental proportions which eventually led to the disclosure. As every good reporter should, Mrs Herlihy added the name to her little list. Her editor said so very often, It doesn't matter whether you say something good or bad about people, just as long as you spell their names right.

'So you and your daughter are going to live in Plymouth after your confirmation?'

'Whoa,' he chuckled. 'That's all a little too soon. There's many a slip, and so forth. Yes, we're going to live in Plymouth, but I have no certain knowledge I'll be confirmed, you know. This is a lovely town. You can quote me. I intend to make America's home town my own.'

'Lovely,' Mrs Herlihy gushed. 'And Valeria, too?'

He was a little slow on the uptake with that one, but Val could feel the steel claws slipping out. 'Oh, you don't want my name mixed up in something important like Mr Thomas's nomination to the Bench. We——'

'Come, come, Valeria,' Mrs Herlihy shook her head sadly. 'That's naughty of you, you know. I saw Mr Thomas come to your house on Monday, and he stayed the night. It's a terrible thing to think of, my dear, when your sins find you out. What would your grandmother have said?'

For about ten seconds Valeria felt like punching the sweet old thing right on her bulbous nose, but sanity won out. 'Sins?' she asked coldly. 'I don't know what you're talking about, Mrs Herlihy. I——'

'I don't know what you're talking about either,' Bart interrupted. 'And although I never knew Valeria's grandmother, I think she would be very tickled. For your information, my fiancée was merely looking after my daughter while I had to be in Boston for some charity work.'

Your what? Valeria screamed to herself. Your fiancée? Me? Why you rotten—— She clamped a hand over her mouth and turned away, just in time to see Maria glaring at her. Hatred. That was the only name applicable. Hatred, spiced with a little disgust, perhaps.

'Your fiancée?' Mrs Herlihy's third pencil had broken. 'Oh, what a scoop this will make! Lovely little Valeria, going to be married. Have you set the date?'

'We've hardly got engaged,' he protested. 'And that's all I can tell you right now. Come and see me in a couple of weeks. Perhaps something new might pop up.'

'Oh, I will,' the reporter simpered. 'And you, Valeria. I've been your next-door neighbour all your young life, and you never thought to tell me! Shame!'

'I—never told *anyone*,' Val returned weakly. *Not even me!* 'It was to be a surprise, you see. I—ah—goodbye, Mrs Herlihy.'

The notebook clicked shut with a snap. Martha Herlihy had triumphed. She offered them all an absent-minded smile, her mind already on her first paragraph, and scuttled up the hill.

'Good God,' Bart Thomas sighed.

'Fiancée!' Valeria snapped at him. 'Of all the goose-brained ideas—you might just as well have called me your mother-in-law!' With both hands on her hips, her cheeks red with embarrassment, her feet slightly spread, she glared up at him.

'I told you not to do that!' Maria stormed into the argument, her fingers poised as little claws. 'I told you not to do anything funny about my father!'

'I don't think this is very funny,' Valeria returned coldly. 'Not funny at all. You could move all the way to Hyannis if you want to—me, I have to make my living in this town.'

'Surely it won't damage your reputation for people to think you were engaged to me,' he objected. 'In fact, I think it might just add a little lustre to your dull life.'

'Why, you pompous——I'll lustre you, you——'

'Don't talk about my dad that way,' Maria interjected, stepping between them with both hands raised.

'Besides, I couldn't think of another damn thing to say,' he concluded regretfully. 'I couldn't let her go out spreading it around that we shared a roof unchaperoned, could I? That sort of suggestion always leads to other things we might possibly have shared, you know. How do you think *that* would sit with the governor's council?'

'Oh, so *that's* it,' Valeria raged. 'It wasn't *my* reputation you were worried about. It was your own! Why you hypocritical, cock-eyed, rotten——'

'Uh—uh—uh,' he chuckled as he waved an admonishing finger. A wide grin spread across his face. 'There are little ears. Besides, it isn't true. My mother and father were definitely married before I was born!'

'Dad, what *are* you two talking about?' Maria asked, agitated by the whole tenor of the conversation.

'Nothing. Just grown-up talk,' her father said gently. 'And I think we'd better get out of here before we gather a crowd. Valeria?' He reached out a hand in her direction.

'I'd sooner hold hands with a rattle-snake,' she muttered. 'Fiancée, indeed!'

'Yes, well, I suppose it does take some getting used to,' he returned briskly. 'I'll increase your pay by twenty per cent. Maria, let's go!'

'Are you *really* gonna marry *her*?' The enraged girl had lost both her cool and grammar. 'I won't ride in the car with *her*, and you can't make me!'

'Don't count on it, child,' he said grimly. 'Get going before I paddle your little round bottom.'

'You wouldn't dare,' she shrieked back at him. 'You— nobody ever paddled me——'

'Then it's about time someone did,' her father assured her. 'Now walk ahead of me, and don't say another word, young lady.' His daughter glared up at him for a moment, decided he really meant it, and went back up Water Street toward the parking area that stretched between the two piers.

'And now it's your turn,' he said gruffly.

'Me?' Valeria demanded. He looked as if he might gladly bite off her head, and all the result of his own stupid statement. But if I try to make a perfectly valid point of it right here, she told herself, he might kill me dead. Or do some other nasty thing! And a twenty per cent pay raise? I never ever made that much money, not in my whole life!

'I'm going,' she muttered. 'And I'm not talking. But I'm thinking, Mr Bartholomew Thomas. And when I get through thinking——'

'I know,' he answered wearily. 'The sky will fall. Well, at least you know your employer's name. Get in the car. We'll fight this thing out when we get home.' One of his hands on her shoulder turned her in the right direction, and a not-altogether-gentle pat on her bottom urged her on.

As a result, the Mercedes made one more of those trips when everyone sat in a neutral corner and not a word was exchanged until they went up the front steps of the house on Cobbs Hollow Lane. At which point he became a dictator.

'You,' he said grimly to his daughter, 'upstairs. It's time you did a little studying. School opens in four weeks around these parts.'

'Six weeks,' Valeria corrected, and then wished she hadn't. His daughter fled the scene, leaving Val alone to face the storm.

'And you, Miss Smartmouth,' he growled, 'into the library. Now.'

She wanted very badly to tell him a number of things. For example, that it couldn't be a library if it had not a single book within its walls. And she was *not* his fiancée, because she couldn't stand the way he combed his hair! But the words all jammed up at the narrow portion of her throat as she watched him stalk down the corridor, anger oozing from every pore. So she followed him, hands folded behind her back, and a most prim little smile on her face.

'Sit!' he commanded.

She sat.

'Now, young lady, I realise that I must have startled you by announcing our engagement.' He stalked up and down in front of her, wearing a narrow rut in the thick pile of the rug. And at each step he banged one of his fists into the palm of the other hand and swore under his breath.

'I—think that's a valid statement,' Val returned nervously. It was *not* excessively warm in the room. Somewhere in the house, air-conditioners hummed. But for some reason she was perspiring madly. Even the palms of her hands were wet.

'Let me explain,' he growled, coming to a stop in front of her. Valeria flinched away from him, moving back until she was rigid against the stuffing of the chair.

'Yes,' she whispered hesitantly, ready to throw herself backward and on to the floor if he moved another inch in her direction. He moved, leaning over her and placing a hand on each of the chair arms to support her. And her muscles were locked up in knots, and would not respond.

'That sweet little old neighbour of yours is trying to do a number on me.' A cold, hard statement of fact, but his mouth was but inches from hers, and the whole thing seemed a threat. What I need, she told herself, is a very large injection of courage. Buck up, woman!

'Yes,' she agreed hurriedly. 'She's that sort of woman.'

'I have a suspicion that your grandmother was not exactly a friend of hers?'

'Not exactly.'

'Dear God,' he muttered. 'You realise she was trying to set us up? The two of us overnight in your house, and obviously up to hanky-panky?'

'I don't know about hanky-panky,' Valeria sighed. 'I think she thought we were in bed and——'

'In the same bed,' he grated. 'That woman could smell a conspiracy from forty miles away. So how would that sit with your friends or the school committee, Miss Brewster?'

'I—my friends wouldn't believe it.' She stopped for a breath, considering the second part of the question carefully. 'The school committee—I just don't know about them. I have tenure. Which means they can't fire me——'

'Except for incompetence or moral turpitude,' he growled. 'Moral turpitude.'

'Could you—no, I guess you couldn't.'

'Could I what?'

'Could you just—give me a little space to breathe?' And then as a desperate addition, 'Please?'

'No, I can't,' he muttered, and closed that last little distance to touch her lips with his own. It was not one of those passionate kisses that sent heroines of the silver screen to writhing and moaning. But it was comfortable, warm, moist, tender, and Valeria relaxed under the gentle ministration. He broke away too soon.

'Damn. I didn't mean to do that,' he muttered as he stepped back a pace. Me neither, she thought happily, but what a wonderful idea. Gran would certainly approve of all this! Her courage restored, she smiled up at him.

'So, Miss Brewster. Engaged people these days are granted a little more latitude than most. By smothering that woman's innuendoes with an engagement ring, I save your reputation—and my own. Two birds with one stone, so to speak.'

'What kind of a stone?' she asked pragmatically.

'What?'

'The stone you used to kill the two birds. That will be in the engagement ring, right?'

'Well, I'll be——' he started to say, but a noise at the door interrupted. Both of them looked in that direction. Amelé Poitras was posed in the doorway, one ample hip braced against the jam, glaring at them both. She stalked into the room.

'Did I hear the words *engagement ring*?' the blonde asked suspiciously.

'Oh, my,' Valeria sighed, trying to sink back out of sight in the chair. Bart Thomas smiled a very thin smile, the kind that—put on a knife-handle—would have made a fine cutting tool.

'I understood that you told a Mrs Herlihy where we were this morning,' he said coldly.

'Of course I did,' Amelé whined. 'You went off and left me alone in this crazy house. What about the engagement ring?'

'Did you know Mrs Herlihy was a reporter?'

'Of course I did,' she returned. 'Everybody knows that. Now what about——'

'Well, in that case,' he said, 'you'll be happy to know that Valeria and I have just become engaged.'

'Don't,' Valeria shouted, jumping to her feet. 'That vase is very valuable!'

Amelé Poitras didn't seem to care about the vase. Since she was explaining herself in very loud, bitter French, the sound of the vase smashing against the wall close to where Bart's head had been provided an excellent translation.

# CHAPTER FIVE

IT WAS warm outside at the pool. A week into August, the steamy dog-days were upon them. Maria, baked to a dusky brown, stretched out on a water-bed on the concrete apron in her one-piece suit, looked twenty-one instead of thirteen. Valeria, a golden girl in her yellow bikini, had taken shelter from the sun under one of the umbrellas, her deep red hair spread out in separate filaments to facilitate the drying. Her clipboard contained half a dozen suggested pamphlets, and her fingers were smudged from her ballpoint pen. The ring she wore was a deep-coloured ruby surrounded by four small diamonds, which increased its fire and sparkle. Even the ink-stains could not hide its slender beauty; not too big, not too little. He had wonderful taste. Probably from lots of experience, Val thought. She had not by any means adapted to this new situation. Neither had Rudolph. He was sprawled out in the minimum shade, panting after his own tree-lined back yard and his own water bowl.

'I'm certainly glad we're on speaking terms,' Val teased the girl. 'It's been a long, dry summer around here with no one to talk to.'

'Well—it's hard to believe your engagement is all make-believe,' Maria said. 'What with that ring, and the local newspaper stories, and all. But I guess it's true. The both of you are only faking it, right?'

'Right,' Val agreed enthusiastically. 'Can you really imagine me being married to your father?'

'He isn't all *that* bad,' Maria returned defensively. 'There's lots of women who like him, you know. I even like him myself!'

'Yes, well I might like him too if I were his daughter,' Val insisted. 'But to be his wife? No chance, lady! How come it took you so long to come around to my side of things?'

'You know what convinced me?' the girl asked rhetorically. 'It was last night when Amelé finally packed up and roared out the door. Anybody who can make that woman disappear must have *something* going for her.'

'Well, thank you,' Val offered demurely. 'And here all along I thought it was my patience, concern and good looks that brought you around!'

'Don't knock it,' Maria announced. 'Two out of three ain't—isn't——?'

'Aren't,' Val suggested.

'Yeah, well, two out of three aren't half bad.' And if I sit here for twenty years, Val thought, she'll never tell me which two I rate well on! The child is daughter of her father, believe me. Two of a kind. Just imagine, if I married that lout I'd have to carry a club around with me to help me win some of the arguments around here!

She shook her head in disgust and went back to her papers. 'How about this for a headline?' she called. '"Power for the people!"'

'Not too brilliant,' the girl laughed. 'Where did you get that corny idea?'

'Well—from your father, actually,' Valeria confessed. 'He offered me two or three titles. Actually, what he said was "Electric power for the people", but I couldn't get that all in one line.'

'You need something more to the point,' Maria giggled. 'How about "Axe the Atom"? Or—what is it they call that place?'

'Pilgrim Station,' Valeria supplied. 'They originally called it Pilgrim I, because they planned to build a second nuclear station next door to it, but we Axed that Atom all right. Say, how about "Unplug the Pilgrim"?'

'Oh, brother!' the girl giggled. 'That's *really* cornball. What you need is a little youth and excitement in your group.'

Val was not *too* insulted by the statement. To a girl of thirteen, anything over twenty-one was going downhill. And her group of volunteers, the women who posted the pamphlets and went door-to-door with their campaign, they did tend to be a little long in the tooth, even to someone of Valeria's age. 'So perhaps we do,' she agreed mildly. 'But I don't intend to ask *you* to volunteer, young lady. I've got enough troubles of my own, you know.'

'I can see that,' the girl mused. 'My dad—he's a very calm guy, but sometimes he loses his temper, and then look out! You know he'll murder you if he finds out what you're doing.' Maria stopped for a second to contemplate the horror. 'You seem to do a lot of skating on thin ice.'

'Everybody has the right to make her views known,' Valeria returned huffily. 'I can't help it if your father isn't in tune with the times! And besides, as long as we're using his machine and his ink and his paper, I thought he deserved to have his *ideas* aired around also. Don't you?'

Maria swam over to the edge of the pool and pulled herself out on to the apron with practised ease. 'I missed that part,' she said, unbelieving. 'You're using Papa's ink and paper and machine to—oh, lord, if he catches up to *that* you'll be swinging in the wind, Valeria. I thought schoolteachers were more—conservative than that!'

I don't see why they should be,' Val defended herself. 'Schoolteachers come in all sizes and shapes and philosophies. And your father won't find out if there aren't any loose lips around the house. And if he does, I can always run and hide. Or something.'

It was as if she had conjured him up. One minute the pair of them were quietly at poolside, having completed their maths lesson for the day, and the next a toy bulldozer came rattling across the lawn, pulling a boat trailer behind it.

'Papa,' the girl squealed. 'Are you driving that thing?' Another score for my side, Val told herself. Not a formal 'father' or 'Daddy' any more. Now it's informal—Papa!

'Of course I'm driving that thing,' he roared back. 'Come see!'

The two women gathered up their paraphernalia and trailed him as he jockeyed the boat trailer and its contents down to the beach and backed it out into the water. 'Now, what do you think that is?' he yelled enthusiastically.

'I—it's a boat?' Valeria hazarded a guess, not too sure herself.

'Of course it's a boat.' He laughed heartily as he climbed up on the trailer and unstrapped the canvas cover. 'It's a catamaran.'

'Why, of course it is,' Val agreed, having no idea what a catamaran might be, but willing to be convinced. Over the course of the past three weeks Bart Thomas had changed. Pomp and circumstance had fled, to be replaced by a loving father, willing to devote a great deal of his time to his daughter. And he had sealed her approval the previous night when he had walked over to the front door, opened it wide, and said, 'Amelé, if you're not happy with us, why don't you just scoot back to your loving father?'

'You don't mean that!' the blonde had exclaimed in surprise. 'You surely don't mean that!' The second part of the sentence had risen to a shrill scream.

'I surely do,' Bart had told her gently. 'You've become a very large pain in the butt, young lady!' And Amelé Poitras had slammed her way out of the house, heading for parts unknown!

Some time later Maria had met Valeria in the hall outside her bedroom door. The girl was clutching a huge stuffed bear, almost as tall as she was—and smiling. 'I'm sure I'm going to sleep well tonight, Valeria,' she had said, her smile big enough to eat up the world.

And Valeria had returned the smile. 'I'm sure *I'm* going to do the same, Maria,' she had responded. And although her Pilgrim conscience had bothered her, since it wasn't exactly the Christian way to do things, nevertheless, she had done just that. Slept like a baby through the night, that was. And now here was Bart Thomas— with a new toy, evidently, and as happy as a turkey at a vegetarian Thanksgiving feast.

'It—doesn't look much like a boat,' Maria suggested.

'Oh, ye of little faith,' her father chuckled. 'It's a shallow-draft sailing catamaran. Two hulls, see there—' He gestured to prove his point. 'And a con- necting deck made out of canvas——' Another gesture. 'And a mast and sails and rudder, and now everybody give a hand here!'

His idea of 'everybody give a hand' would have ranked well with Simon LeGree and the slave mansions. Valeria on one side, and Maria on the other, were handed ropes and told to pull, while he resumed his lordly seat on the bulldozer and gently teased the trailer out from under the hull of the boat. Or rather, two hulls.

'That's great,' he rumbled as he climbed down to join them. 'A fine job.' He looked with appreciation as the twenty-foot craft bobbed in the shallow water.

'Yes, we should do this every day,' Val said sarcastically, looking at the blister forming in the palm of her hand.

'Oh, no,' he objected grandly. 'We only need to do it once.' He patted his daughter on the head and kissed Val on her forehead. 'Once a season, that is. We're going to have a grand time sailing up and down the harbour. It's good for my image.'

'There's one small problem,' Valeria interjected cautiously. 'Does anyone present know *how* to sail a boat?'

'What's to know?' he laughed. 'The boat rests on top of the water, the wind blows in the sail, and *voilà*!'

Good lord, Val thought, have I found his weakness? He knows beans about sailing! The harbour is full of sand bars and mud flats, and a rock or two, and this legal beagle is going to—oh, well, what's the difference? The worst he can do is run us up on a rock, and at low tide we can all walk home!

'There are a—few rules,' she suggested, doing her best to hide the giggles. 'The coastguard is pretty strict in these parts.'

'Not to worry. I bought a book.' And so he had. He waved it in front of her eyes. A big, official-looking book, with pictures, she was glad to note. 'And I read it last night. Now then, let's get the mast steeped, and——'

'Stepped,' Val corrected. 'The mast gets stepped.' He gave her a stern look, as if his dignity were at stake.

'Stepped—steeped—what difference does it make? We put the stick in that hole up in front, and that's all there is to it, right?'

'Right,' Maria agreed. She gave him a big, sunny smile. Valeria did too, as she checked around to see where the life preservers were located.

Putting 'that stick in the hole' wasn't as easy as he had suggested. When Harry came down from the house with a lunch basket, the mast was still unstepped. But the wizened little man seemed to know a little bit about everything, and with his help the ship was quickly rigged.

'I could have done it easily myself,' Bart boasted as he bit into one of Mabel's ham sandwiches, 'but with only female helpers—well, you know how it is.'

'Indeed I do,' Valeria returned, with just a little touch of sarcasm. 'I'm too old to be influenced, but you're giving your daughter a good case of inferiority, talking like that.'

'Am I really?' He acted as if the thought had never crossed his mind. But his daughter evidently knew something that Val did not. The girl was working on a peanut butter and jelly sandwich, and her big smile broke up the conversation.

'Oh, Papa,' she admonished. 'Stop teasing.' He grinned, she grinned back at him, and Valeria was left to wonder just what dandy little secret had escaped her.

They launched the boat at one o'clock. A misnomer that he insisted on, even when Valeria pointed out that it was already afloat. And the christening didn't work quite right. Mabel refused to sacrifice a glass bottle. Maria did her best with a paper carton of orange juice, but it wasn't exactly the same. Bart was still grumbling as he shoved off from the dock.

The mainsail had gone up with no trouble at all. It had already been set at the second reef, but there was enough wind to push the boat ahead at a good clip. Beginner's luck, Val thought as she huddled up near the mast and watched. The tide was approaching the high-water mark. There were a number of spots in the harbour, she knew, that were marked on the harbour chart as having only one foot in depth at the mean low tide. So he had a chance to pile them up in grand style even before they cleared the sheltering arm of Plymouth Beach Peninsula.

'How much water does this—boat draw?' she asked as he settled back at the helm. He grinned at her, and his daughter wore the same sort of face.

'Six inches,' he reported. 'I read the charts before I bought the boat. You didn't think I was smart enough for that, did you?'

'I—to be truthful, no,' she said directly. Strange, how different he looked, balancing himself against the slight chop that struck them the minute they reached the open bay between Plymouth Peninsula and Saquish Neck. Confidence. That was the word that fitted. Altogether confident. The catamaran began to heel slightly as the off-shore wind picked up. The clear, cool smell of the sea assaulted her nostrils, that salt and iodide kiss that washed away all the odours of the land.

He was kneeling beside the tiller, making casual small adjustments, his eye on the throat of the sail. He looked so—qualified. And even in his curious garb—a tiny pair of trunks just covering the essentials, and the orange life-jacket barely able to reach over his chest—he looked dignified. If that were the proper word?

'Papa, stop teasing her,' Maria yelled from her perch on the bow.

'Me? Tease?'

'Oh, brother,' the girl muttered as she worked her way back across the pitching deck to where Valeria sat. 'Men!' she said disgustedly.

'I agree heartily,' Val said. 'As a generality, that is. What's the secret?'

'He's been a sailor for a long time,' Maria said glumly. 'He was in the Navy for a little while, too, you know.'

Val glared at him. Her little advantage had crumbled into nothing. Not only that, but he must have *known* what she was thinking, and then he played up to it—and her—as if he had hooked a fish on his line. Just exactly the way he had hooked her on his line with that bit about the engagement! Damn the man!

'Why don't you go back up in the bow?' she yelled in the girl's ear. 'I want to massacre your father!'

'Why not?' Maria gave her an exaggerated wink and slid cautiously forward again.

Just as cautiously Val made her way to the stern and sat down on the other side of the tiller from him. They had just swung on to an east-northeasterly course, and the boom had rattled over, inches from her head.

'You're supposed to give some sort of warning,' she told him angrily. 'I could have had my head knocked off.'

'Why, I believe I did,' he returned, and the surprised look on his face made her realise that he probably had—but in her angry self-examination she had completely missed the signal. But that's not going to make me feel better, she told herself. I'm angry with the man. I intend to continue to be angry with the man. And as long as I'm angry, he's going to know about it!

'I hear tell that you're a fake,' she began. He spared her a quick look. At the same moment the old blue Alice band she had used to fasten her hair gave up the ghost

and went whirling down the wind. Her beautiful hair
scattered in all directions, blinding her.

'Hey,' he said softly. She could hear and sense the awe
in his voice. 'I have never in my life seen anything like
that, Valeria.'

Soft soap, she told herself firmly. Disregard. He's a
wolf in wolf's clothing. 'I'm told that you've been a
yachtsman for years,' she stated. 'And that you've been
having me on, Mr Thomas. If that's your real name!'

'As a matter of fact, it isn't,' he laughed. It was a
laugh full of the joy and excitement of life—of young
life. Val could hardly suppress the little shiver that ran
up her spine.

'But I never thought you'd find me out,' he continued. 'My great-grandfather came over from Poland
at the turn of the century. Our real family name is
Thomazieski, but the Immigration people couldn't
handle anything over six letters—so—Thomas.'

Valeria managed to get her hair under control by the
simple expedient of grabbing it in both hands and
holding on for dear life. 'Move over a little,' he called,
and loaned a hand to help her. 'Now, hold still. I've got
an extra shoelace here.' Her back was to him, and when
she turned her head to see what was going on he roared
at her.

'Be still, damn it!' He was balancing the force of the
tiller with one knee, and with the other lacing her hair
into a ponytail, using his shoelace. When the operation
was over, the tiller was still between them, but her hip
touched his, his arm was around her shoulders, and
Valeria very suddenly felt—small? Comforted? Warmed?

He won't get away with all that so easily, she promised
herself. I'd think it was lust he's working at, but who
the devil can find anything sexy about a girl wrapped
up in a stuffed life-jacket, all wet from the spray

bouncing over the forward quarter? Every bit of her make-up had long since washed away, her hair flew like a pennant at half-mast behind her and—— *I'm still angry with him. Very darn angry!* The sun sparkled from her ring-finger, and gave her new fuel for the fire.

'It's been a while since that awful Mrs Herlihy wrote that story for the local paper,' she began.

It got his full attention. He brought the boat around into the wind, and let it sit there in stays while he examined her face very carefully. 'I suppose so,' he said. She could feel the weight of his caution. Three words, all carefully neutral, all carefully selected.

'And I don't see any reaction,' she continued doggedly. 'It didn't get picked up by the Boston papers, and nobody has raised a ruckus about our little—escapade.'

'Perhaps,' he muttered, taking a quick look around. They were right in the middle of the channel, but Plymouth Harbour was perhaps not the busiest little port in the world. It was too small for the Mayflower to penetrate in 1620, and since then it hadn't got any more seaworthy. 'Perhaps,' he repeated. 'Is this all leading up to something?'

'What's going on?' Maria yelled from her position in the bow.

'I'm resting the boat,' he yelled back. 'I ran it too fast and it's tired. Besides which, Miss Brewster and I are talking about your birthday party, and we don't care to have you know all our secrets!'

Maria shook her head sadly and laughed. Boat-resting she understood as foolishness; birthday parties and secrets were another matter, one which no sensible birthday girl would want to interrupt. So she waved a hand in acknowledgement and turned back to her study of the party of seagulls dive-bombing their wake, looking for a refreshing meal of garbage.

'Now, then,' he repeated. 'What's all this leading up to?'

Valeria gulped a deep breath, got a firm grip on herself, and started to explain. 'I think that whole fuss has all blown over. I don't think there's any chance now of our little overnight arrangement interfering with your confirmation. So—I think that it's time we called an end to this fake engagement. Your daughter finds it very hard to believe. Mabel finds it very easy to believe and keeps pushing me to tell her the wedding date. Every time Harry walks past he keeps giving me one of those knowing little winks. And every time I pass a mirror I see a woman glaring at me, asking just what the devil I'm doing, lying my soul away right out in plain public sight!'

'Well, that *is* a handful,' he commented. 'Watch it, I'm about to come about.' He pulled the tiller toward him, and the boat began to fall away into the wind. For several minutes he was absorbed in the manoeuvre, bringing the boat up to speed, running before the wind now, back toward the harbour.

It was a cool casual movement to accomplish a fairly difficult manoeuvre, but as he worked with rudder and sheets she studied his face and arrived at the firm conviction that he was stalling, trying to think of something to say. And she arrived at something more. For some stupid reason, she was sorry she had brought up the whole affair. He might decide indeed to call the whole engagement off, and, despite what she had just told him, she would rather *not* end it. A silly conclusion, but there it was. Maybe it's the ring, she told herself. I love that ring, but I'd have to give it back if we're not—lord, what a mess!

'You have a good point there,' he finally said. Her heart dropped clear through her shoes, and another cold shiver ran up her spine. 'But there are some little difficulties.'

'Oh,' she managed weakly, and felt instantly better as his arm tightened around her shoulders. The solid oak of the tiller arm dug into her side, but it was a small discomfort to pay for the greater advantage.

'Yes,' he continued. 'In a couple of days there's a gathering of the Old Colony Club. A small dinner. I've been invited to join them, and say a few words. It's for couples. They'll all expect me to bring my fiancée along.'

'The Old Colony Club?' she gasped. 'Founded in 1769? The Winslows, the Lothrops, the Watsons? Sam Adams? And Thomazieski?'

'They don't know about *that*,' he laughed. 'One of the founders of the club was John Thomas. Maybe they think I'm related? That's not important. What *is* important is that I'll need to have you with me then. You *do* understand?'

No, I don't, she wanted to say, but held back. It couldn't really make much difference, this two- or three-day extension. The whole thing is getting to be so much like a Cinderella story that I hate to think of going back to cleaning up the ashes after it's over, she thought. Or back to schoolteaching. Isn't that strange? I've only ever wanted to be a schoolteacher, and now suddenly it doesn't seem to be all that important any more!

'Yes, I guess it wouldn't be any trouble—for a few more days,' she said.

'Good,' he said, and gave her a robust pat on the back that almost fractured her spine. 'Now, go forward there and watch how skilfully I come up to the dock.'

'And Mabel, you wouldn't believe how skilfully he came up to the dock,' Valeria said between the giggles. They were all at the table for supper. Bart, still casually dressed in black trousers and white shirt, his hair wet from a shower. Maria, in a neat little orange-blossom sun-dress, with her hair brushed until it gleamed, braided and pinned up in the mode that Valeria herself wore. Mrs Baines, in a high-necked dress of soft grey cotton that managed to cling to her angular figure, sharing the meal but jumping up and down like a jumping-jack to fetch and carry. And Valeria, in a pale rose, off-the-shoulder blouse and skirt, two years old now, but still fashionable. For the first time since Gran's funeral, Valeria's dress fitted her figure. Eating too much, girl, she had chided herself when she'd put it on.

Everything is just the slightest bit—but what the heck! It felt good—and she felt good. And after she had helped Maria with her hair, Val had brushed her own dark mane and braided it up into a coronet. For no good reason, of course. At least, none she was willing to admit.

'Save it until Harry comes back from his errand,' Maria suggested. Her father glared at them both. No sense of humour? Val asked herself. Well, if he's going to be a judge he needs one—and I appoint myself the Chairwoman of the Humour Board!

'I'll tell Harry later.' She smiled at Bart from across the table length. His lips twitched, but that steely look still rode in his eyes. 'It'll sound better the second time around.'

'So go ahead,' Mabel Baines encouraged. 'That's the last of the dishes and I'm ready to listen!'

'So we came up the harbour with the wind off our port beam,' Val started out mischievously. 'Maria and I were standing in the bow, ready to secure, you know. He came south past the dock, luffed up without any warning, and we were hung up in stays again, with the tide going out.'

'Now that wasn't the way I remember it,' Bart interjected.

'Well, this is *my* story,' Valeria insisted. 'You can tell your own story afterwards. Anyway, he finally got the boat to fall off the wind, got up a little speed, and came around again. All very neat and tidy, on the south side of the dock—and we ran aground! Maria and I went——'

'We went overboard,' Maria laughed. 'Right off the bow!'

'Why, that's terrible,' Mrs Baines said, alarmed. 'You must have been hurt?'

'Not a bit,' Val laughed. 'We landed feet first in two inches of water, and walked ashore.'

'Leaving me to struggle to get the boat moored,' Bart complained mournfully. 'They stood on the beach, the pair of them, and laughed their fool heads off. But there'll be a reckoning some day, let me assure you.'

'You couldn't expect us to walk back out and get wet again,' his daughter exclaimed. 'And it was so funny——'

'Yeah, funny,' her father declared, and then the solemn look faded and a huge grin broke out. Val, who had been holding her breath, unable to decide how he would take the whole thing, relaxed with a vast sigh of relief. 'But what you don't know,' he assured them all, 'was that I intended to ground the boat at just that spot. It had a nice sandy bottom, the tide was running out, it was protected from winds up the harbour, and I didn't have any fenders aboard to keep from scratching up the hull if I had come alongside the dock. This ice-cream is delicious, Mabel. Home-made?'

'Oh, yes,' the housekeeper said. 'Right off the super-market shelves.'

'But Valeria didn't tell——' Maria started to complete the story, her eyes wide with laughter, but Harry came in at just that moment with some newspapers in his hand. There were worry lines on the little man's face. He nodded to Bart, but said not a word. The grin on Bart's face faded completely, and for a moment he hesitated. Then he picked up his napkin from his lap, dabbed at his lips, and pushed his chair back.

'I think that Maria and I have to have a short talk,' he sighed. Harry brought the newspapers over to him and pointed out one section on the first page. 'And maybe you'd better join us, Valeria, please.'

A look of puzzled expectancy had wiped the laughter out of Maria's face. Val shook her head. Only in the last week had the girl pulled herself out of her forlorn stage; laughter was not a product much in use in her young life. Bart rose silently, held his daughter's chair for her, and the two of them trailed off down the hall toward the library. Valeria hesitated, looking at Harry for some guidance. The little man's face was fixed in stone. He came over and held her chair, nodding in the direction the others had gone.

'Oh, dear,' Mabel Baines muttered as she snatched at a few of the dirty dishes and fled toward the kitchen. 'I hadn't expected it so soon.'

As puzzled as Maria had been, Valeria got up slowly, holding her napkin for a moment as she reflected, and then dropped it on the table and hurried to join the Thomas family.

Bart was behind the big desk in the library, drumming his fingers on its highly polished top. 'Shut the door,' he ordered as Valeria came in. Maria was sitting uneasily in the big upholstered chair beside the desk. The newspapers were under Bart's hand. He gestured Val into a chair beside Maria.

'I have some news from California,' he started out. His voice was deep and gentle as he eyed his daughter.

'Something's happened to my mother!' The girl jumped up from her chair, fists clenched, a tear forming in the corner of each eye.

'I don't know any good way to put this,' her father said slowly. He offered an arm, and his daughter moved into its shelter, standing beside his chair and resting her head against his. 'Something has happened to your mother, yes. But it isn't necessarily bad, love. Eleanore— your mother—has married Mr Stanhope, the movie producer. Yesterday, evidently, but the story just got to the East Coast today.'

'No! I don't believe it!' The sobs that shook Maria's frame were dry, hurtful. She buried her face in her father's hair. 'I don't believe it. She wouldn't do that to me! She wouldn't!' And then the tears started.

Valeria, undecided, stood up and took a step in their direction, but over the girl's bowed head Bart made a negative signal. He let the girl cry for a time.

'You mustn't think of it as something she's done to *you*,' he coaxed. 'Your mother had her own life to lead, my dear. Just now it must have seemed very important to her to marry. Neither you nor I can stand in the way of something like this, Maria. We shouldn't blame her— we should congratulate her and wish her happiness. Perhaps you and I could arrange a telephone call tonight, just to do that?'

The girl freed herself from his arm and moved away a pace. 'I still don't believe it,' she muttered bitterly.

'Look here.' Her father put the newspaper in front of her and pointed to the story. As she slowly read, the shocked disbelief on Maria's face faded, crumbled away, to be replaced by such a look of loss that Valeria could not contain herself any longer. She took another step, and hugged the child.

But Maria would have none of that. 'It's *your* fault,' she snarled at Val. 'It's all *your* fault. If you had let my father alone, this wouldn't have happened. But no, you had to get engaged, didn't you? And my mother heard about it and she got desperate, and so she married that— that wimp! It's all your fault!' The tears were gone. Open warfare glared out of those deep eyes, so much venom that Valeria stepped back in shocked surprise.

'Damn you!' the child screamed. She punched wildly at Val's stomach, and then crammed both fists into her mouth and ran from the room. They could hear the screams echoing down the long hall for endless seconds. The quiet in the library hung like a black, dismal fog.

'Maybe—maybe I'd better go to her,' Valeria stammered.

'No. It wouldn't do any good at this stage,' he returned solemnly. 'Don't take what she said too hard. She's upset, and needs someone to blame.'

'And then again, maybe she's right,' Val said softly. 'Maybe it's just exactly the way she put it!'

'Don't you believe that for a minute,' he commanded. The chair squeaked and he was in front of her, moving like some jungle animal. 'If there's any blame, it belongs to Eleanore and me, no one else.'

His arms came around her as they had come around the child, warm, strong, protective. But Valeria was feeling all the guilt in the world piling up on her shoulders, and could not stifle her own tears. Weeping, she relaxed against him, feeling his muscles take up her weight as if it were nothing, nestling her head against the second button of his soft shirt.

'There, there now,' he murmured into the shining crown of her hair, and although she could not see or feel it, she could have sworn that he kissed the top of her head.

# CHAPTER SIX

'SHE's been in her room for twenty-four hours,' Mabel Baines told Valeria as the pair of them stood in the upstairs hall outside Maria's room. 'She screamed death and destruction at her father, and she threw a glass at me—and missed. So that leaves only you. You know how she eats—like a horse. She hasn't touched a thing all that time, so she really *must* be sick.'

'Fasting wouldn't do her any harm. Not just for twenty-four hours. I don't mind trying, but I think she hates me worse than the rest of you.' Valeria looked down at herself. Jeans and an old flannel shirt with the sleeves rolled up. Bare feet, hair hanging in two braids down her back. What have I got to lose? she thought. I'm about as decrepit as I can possibly get.

'So take this.' Mabel thrust a covered dish at her. 'Chicken soup. It might not do any good, but it couldn't hurt. She hasn't eaten a thing since last night, and here it is, four o'clock in the afternoon already. Cry! Lord, I've never seen a child cry so hard and so long.'

'It's important,' Valeria commented glumly. 'Her whole little world came tumbling down when her mother remarried. Well, I'll give it a try. Where is Bart—er— Mr Thomas, by the way?'

'In the best male tradition, he's down hiding in the library with a bottle of brandy,' the housekeeper chuckled. 'Big, brave, courageous, but when his daughter cries he doesn't know what to do!'

'Me, neither.' Val accepted the deep soup dish, balancing it carefully to avoid burning her hand. What am

I letting myself in for this time? she asked herself. I've let her father con me into this engagement game, and now I need to convince his daughter that she loves me— or at least that she doesn't really want to kill me! And why? For a person raised on logic, I'm certainly becoming a crazy mixed-up kid myself. You'd almost think that I—no, that's not possible. I don't even *like* the guy.

'The dish is too hot?' Mabel looked curiously at her. 'Well, you were sort of staring off into space like that, and I thought that maybe——'

'No, the dish isn't too hot,' Valeria assured her, and reached for the doorknob. No, it isn't the *dish* that's too hot, it's this whole environment that I've got myself trapped in! The latch clicked. Valeria turned around and backed into the door, forcing it open with one rounded buttock. The sobbing behind her stopped as she turned around to face the bed. Behind her, Mabel closed the door. It thumped shut with a definite sound of finality.

Maria looked absolutely tiny as she huddled up in the middle of the king-sized bed. Tiny and dishevelled, her nose a bright red, her eyes tear-swollen, and a suspicious look on her plump little face. Valeria studied her. For once, the child looked her age. Her hair was a mess; she was still wearing her plain cotton nightgown. If misery loves company, Val thought, I've come to the right place. She walked across the room and set the soup-dish down on the night table without saying a word about it.

'What do *you* want?' the child snarled. At least no screams, and no flying objects either, Val told herself as she settled into a chair by the head of the bed. 'Well, don't just sit there.' Maria sat up in the middle of the bed, cross-legged, like a little Buddha. But not so plump as she was two weeks ago, Val thought. Our little exercise programme, plus monitored eating, has done a little something for her. Plus considerable misery and woe! The girl glared at her, and repeated her statement.

Valeria settled herself carefully into the chair and stared out the window for a moment. And then, as if talking to the window, said, 'When my mother became ill, I was about seven years old. She just lay in her bed. She wouldn't speak to me, or play games, or—or anything. And I thought she hated me. I thought the whole world was designed just to give me a hard time. So I was nasty to everybody—including my mother.' She stopped to consider, crossing her right leg over her left and holding on to the right shoe. Out of the corner of her eye she could see that Maria was paying attention.

'And then one night my mother died,' she continued gently. 'Just like that. One minute she was asleep, and the next she was gone. You wouldn't believe how stupid I was. I thought she had died just to spite me. Can you imagine that? It was weeks before I understood—and then it was too late—too late to tell her how much I loved her. Too late to tell her I knew what a fool I'd been. Too late.'

'Oh, God,' the girl muttered under her breath.

'I spent a lot of years recovering from my own idiocies,' Val continued in her low, soft voice. 'My dad was killed a year after my mother died. If it hadn't been for my gran I would have—well, I don't know what I would have done. But Gran taught me something. Mothers and fathers are not *just* parents, they're also themselves. They're real people. They have their own pains and problems and solutions, separate from their children's lives.'

'You mean—like my mother,' Maria rasped.

'Like your mother,' Val agreed. 'Your mother needed someone else in her life. And so she married. It has nothing to do with the way she loves you—nothing.'

'You're just saying that because you want to marry my father,' Maria said bluntly. 'That's what it's all about, isn't it? My mother gets married to that—wimp; you get married to my father—and what about me? Are you planning to send me away to a boarding-school or something?'

'Whatever gave you *that* idea?' Valeria studied the little face, buried in its miseries.

''Cause that's what my mother said. She was going to send me off to a school, and I called Dad, and he came and got me. And now he's gonna do the same thing!'

'I don't have any idea what your father is going to do.' Valeria nibbled at her lower lip and did some fast thinking. 'I don't think he would have gone to all that trouble just to do the very same thing. Besides, you know that your father's engagement to me is a fake. Tonight we go to the dinner at the Old Colony Club, and after that the masquerade is finished. By this time tomorrow you and your father will have this little world to yourselves. Doesn't that make you feel better?'

'But I——' The tears gradually stopped. The child stabbed at her eyes, using the corner of the pillowcase to dry them. 'I'm a fool,' she said bitterly. 'And now I suppose you're going to cuddle up to me and tell me to be a big girl and—like that!'

'Not me,' Val said coolly as she stood up and brushed down her shirt-front. 'The only thing I've got to tell you is *eat your soup*. Mabel is worried about you.' And then, without looking back, Valeria walked to the door. 'Oh, by the way,' she said over her shoulder as she turned the doorknob, 'your father loves you very much.'

There was no explosion from within the room as she closed the door behind her, and an hour later, as she searched her meagre wardrobe for a dress proper enough to suit a dinner with her fiancée, Mabel stuck her head around the doorjamb with a big smile on her face. 'She ate it all,' the housekeeper reported. 'You are some kind of crazy lady, Miss Valeria Brewster!'

I am that, Val laughed to herself as she went in to the shower. Crazy, that was. Anyone in her right mind would have fled the premises days ago! She laughed at herself in the bathroom mirror as she dropped her robe on the floor. Valeria Brewster. Five foot two, give or take a cheating ruler. Green eyes, with such a sparkle in them. Now, what would make my eyes sparkle on an evening like this? Heavy maroon hair, with a light streak or two, bleached by the hot summer sun. Skin that tans lightly, and leaves a trail of almost invisible freckles across my nose. If he ever got close enough, he know about that sort of imperfection. He was a man who wanted only the perfect. *Get out of my mind, Bart Thomas!*

A pert little nose, with the hint of a dimple on each cheek. Smooth, soft shoulders, high apple-breasts. Crab-apples, she snorted. Not worth the bother. Hardly a handful apiece. A girl didn't have to be all that experienced to know what American men liked! She turned her back firmly on the mirror, and then stole a look over her shoulder at the well-shaped legs, the swelling hips, the narrow waist. Funny, with all those imperfections, the whole didn't look too bad. Not at all. She was grinning as she stepped into the shower.

'That's a pretty conservative outfit,' Bart murmured in her ear as they went into the lobby of the motel. Valeria arched her eyebrows at him and stalked ahead toward the restaurant where the dinner was being given. So it wasn't gaudy. None of her clothes were. Everything she owned was geared toward schoolteaching, parent-teacher conferences, school committee meetings. But this dress was none of those. This one was designed to show maturity, purpose, concern, dignity. She had bought it strictly for those appearances in court—when it was time to impress a male judge with the idea that not all female protesters were mad! Court appearances that had, unfortunately, been more and more frequent these latter days!

And so here she was in her neat little basic black dress. The one that buttoned up the front to the white Peter Pan collar with little pearl shell fasteners, clung close to her above the waist, and flared out gently below, until it hovered just exactly at her knees. As befitting a summer dress, it floated in all its silken glory, a thin shell that required a full-length petticoat beneath it lest there be more of Valeria Brewster on display than there was dress. With her hair up in a sophisticated swirl, her mother's pearls around her neck, and a minimum of lipstick and mascara, she was ready for the war to begin.

The first gun was fired at the door to the restaurant. 'Ah, Mr Thomas!' Valeria's head snapped up. She knew that voice too well. 'I'm Peterson, the chief of Police.' His hand extended, Chief Mal Peterson fitted his dinner jacket like a tub fits a firkin of butter. 'And look who you have with you! Little Valeria!'

Bart shook the extended hand and smiled down at Val. 'You and the chief are acquainted?'

'Of course,' she sighed. 'His was one of my references. You *do* remember, don't you?'

'Can't say that I do,' Bart laughed. 'I never did get around to reading them. We're sharing a table, Chief?'

'Right up there on the dais,' the chief returned as he escorted them both down the length of the room. 'Have to treat our newest judge with respect, you know.'

'Not yet,' Bart chuckled. 'There's still a distance to go—what was that old cliché?'

'Many a slip 'twixt cup and lip,' Valeria prodded. There were empty chairs at the head table, and places reserved. Lights were focused on the dais, making it difficult to see the rest of the audience. And here I am, she thought. Identification parade. Who's that woman with the new judge? His fiancée? Looks more like the Brewster woman. You know, the one who——

'I suppose, this being your home town, you know all about my fiancée,' Bart said over the din. Chief Peterson almost choked over his shrimp cocktail.

'Know about her?' he asked incredulously. 'You couldn't find another person in the county who knows as much about the Brewsters as I do.'

'I'm sure Bart doesn't want to hear about old sins,' Valeria interjected nervously. Her hand jittered so badly that the shrimp fell off her fork on to the plate of ice.

'I'm sure he does,' Bart insisted. 'Old sins, old passions. Anything. For all the time I've known her, Valeria is pretty darn quiet about her past!'

'I don't think——' she started to say.

'Listen, it's a great story,' the chief chuckled, having finished his cocktail. 'Let me tell you about the Pot-hole Bandit!'

Valeria, who had hardly made a dent in *her* entrée, put her fork down. Her fingers were no longer capable of holding it. 'That's not fair,' she complained. 'That wasn't——'

'Let me tell the story,' the chief insisted. Bart took possession of one of Valeria's hands, and squeezed it gently. 'Behave like a fiancée,' he whispered in her ear. 'Look at me adoringly! Well, look at me, at least!'

'I can't,' she whispered back. 'I think I'm going to throw up!'

'It started about five years ago,' the chief reminisced. 'That was a cold winter. When spring came there were all sorts of holes in the roads. We call them pot-holes up here. Somehow or another they didn't get fixed very rapidly. Accusations were made that only streets where council members lived got fixed. So all of a sudden the Pot-hole Bandit appeared on the scene. Once a week this bandit would designate a pot-hole that was long overdue for fixing, and on some dark night would plant flowers and bushes in it. Raised hell with the street traffic, it did. The Department of Public Works had to get right on the fix-up, let me tell you. It became a terrible public embarrassment, and the council ordered us to find the guilty party, hang him, and *then* give him a fair trial!'

'I take it you found him?' Bart asked. It was Valeria's turn to choke on the food. The waiters had brought in the bromide of all American political dinners: fried chicken. The chief stopped to take a bite or two.

'I go to these affairs two—three times a week,' Peterson said, waving a drumstick in the air in Bart's direction. 'I keep telling myself beforehand, eat something before you go. But I never learn. Yeah, we caught the Bandit.'

'That wasn't——' Valeria tried to say, but the two men left not a splinter of space for her to speak.

'After six months, we caught the Bandit,' the chief chuckled. 'Tried to overdo it. At the last hole, the Bandit planted a six-foot Christmas tree, complete with ornaments, but his truck broke down, and we finally caught up—with *her*.'

'It wasn't me!' Valeria protested.

'A woman?' Bart said.

'A woman,' the chief agreed. 'An eighty-one-year-old woman.'

'It was my gran,' Valeria sighed. 'I don't know why people keep bringing up that story. My gran never hurt a fly.'

'No, she never did,' the chief mused. 'Sweet, stubborn, sincere. A lot like her grand-daughter. A schoolteacher, too, by the way.'

'Well, nobody's guilty until found so in open court,' Val insisted firmly. 'So Gran was not guilty. Nobody ever found her guilty in court!'

'Caught red-handed, you say, Chief?' Bart drawled. That teasing little smile was playing around his mouth.

'Caught red-handed,' the chief replied solemnly. 'Took her to district court. Eighteen counts of malicious mischief. Four counts of obstruction of a public way. Pictures. Eye-witnesses. Lord, we were the laughing stock of the state.'

'With all that proof?'

'It had nothing to do with the proof,' Valeria interrupted. 'There was no trial.'

'What could you expect?' the chief sighed. He had been laughing so hard that tears had come to his eyes. 'Miz Brewster taught high school for forty years in these parts. There wasn't a judge or clerk or jury anywhere in four counties who hadn't been a student of hers.'

'And they all disqualified themselves from hearing the trial,' Valeria said proudly. 'The case was dismissed six times, and the county commissioners refused to have it brought to trial again.'

'And that's not all,' the chief chuckled. 'When the final decision was taken, the local newspaper ran a campaign in support of Miz Brewster, and they collected something like three thousand dollars, and damned if they didn't award it to her, with a certificate, for being a "concerned citizen"!'

'It was a lovely time,' Val interjected. 'I was always so proud of my gran!'

'And I suppose that's why you took up the protest banner yourself?' the chief asked.

'This is very good ice-cream cake,' Val said hurriedly. 'They make the best in——'

'Oh, I know all about Valeria's activities,' Bart said jovially. 'I've even helped her out with one or two slogans for her pamphlets.'

'Well, now, have you ever?' Chief Peterson's eyebrows rose. Val very indelicately stuck her tongue out—just the slightest bit—at him, and went back to her ice-cream.

'You approve of her nuclear stand?' the chief started to say. But that was the moment when the master of ceremonies stood up, introduced Bart Thomas, and he had to "sing for his supper". On the way home, driven now in his own sleek grey Cadillac, he was all joviality.

'Fine crowd,' he commented, loosening his shirt collar. 'Laughed in all the right places. So your grandmother was the Pot-hole Bandit, was she? I can see it didn't run in the family.'

'No, I guess it didn't,' Valeria returned, snuggling tiredly into the soft upholstery. And then, for some unthinking reason she asked, 'Could you love someone like that?'

'Of course,' he chuckled. 'Your grandfather did, didn't he?'

'Yes,' Val said thoughtfully, 'but he sometimes lived life with a pained expression on his face. He was one of the judges, you see.'

Mabel Baines was sprawled out in the living-room when they arrived, rubbing a compound on her arthritic knuckles. 'Hey,' she said. 'This growing old isn't all it's cracked up to be. If you want my personal opinion, don't! Stay young somehow. Monkey glands, whatever. Have a good time?'

'Great!' Bart said explosively. 'Fine political exposure. And I learned a lot about the natives.'

'I'm hungry,' Valeria interjected quickly, hoping to avoid resuscitation of certain sensitive subjects. 'You could starve to death on that rubber chicken.'

'I'll get you something cold,' the housekeeper promised, scrambling to her feet. 'Dress looks nice, Valeria. What natives did he learn about?'

'I don't know,' Val started to say.

'The Brewsters,' he chortled. 'Did you know they were an old Plymouth family? Came over on the Mayflower. Lord, that must have been one giant of a ship.'

'I don't come from that branch of the family,' Valeria insisted firmly. 'My ancestors came over from Lancaster during the great migration of mill workers in the 1890s. And you needn't spread all you learned all over the countryside.' She gave him a stern look, the kind that could quell riots in the twelfth grade, but evidently made no impression on corporation lawyers.

'Ah, but I enjoy spreading a little gossip,' he chuckled. 'Mabel, did you know that Valeria here is related to the great Pot-hole Bandit of Plymouth?'

'Is she really?' Mrs Baines asked. 'Imagine that, a celebrity right in our midst. I'll get that snack for you.'

'Right in our midst,' he repeated softly. She hated that grin. It was altogether too chauvinistic. He needed taking down a peg or two—but Valeria had no idea how to go about it. So instead of rapier wit she substituted a cold shoulder turned in his direction as she walked over to the sofa.

'That won't do,' he said as he followed her. His weight sank the cushions, and left her sitting on the sliding edge of an abyss—a slide that could only end up against his solid frame. 'You and I have a considerable number of things to talk about, young lady.'

She struggled up the incline to the farthest end of the sofa, and clung there with one hand wrapped desperately around the mahogany arm-rest. Her ring sparkled in the light of the floor-lamp. 'Yes, we do,' she said. Time to attack. Time to show him that not every girl in the world is a push-over for his magnetic tactics. Time to teach him a lesson! She cleared her throat, set both feet precariously down flat on the floor, and glared at him.

'I think I've fulfilled my agreement,' she said stormily. It had to be in anger, or I'll never get it said, she assured herself. 'The party's over. I think I gave good and faithful service as your fiancée, but now there's no sense dragging it along like some little game. So as of this moment, Mr Thomas, we are unengaged. Here.' She slipped his ring off her finger and tendered it in the middle of her palm.

'Just like that?' he mused. 'It couldn't wait until a bright tomorrow?' She pushed the ring a little closer to him, her whole arm trembling.

'Tomorrow *will* be brighter,' she answered angrily. 'Your daughter will love the idea, I'll be relieved of a terrible load of lies, and—I think, deep down, you'll like it a lot yourself! Please take the ring.'

'You know, I really meant for you to keep the ring, no matter what the outcome.' He picked it up with two delicate fingers, turning if from side to side so that spurts of reflected light dazzled her eyes. That's why I want to cry, she told herself bitterly. The reflection's making my eyes water. Damn the man!

'It's really not good form for former fiancées to keep the ring,' she sighed. Why does my finger feel so darn—naked? The stone was too big for a working girl, and I—don't have a bit of affection wrapped up in it—so why do I——

'Oh, hell,' she muttered as two perfect tears, one in each eye, slipped their moorings and tracked down through the scanty powder base on her cheeks. She struggled to get up, but the inclined cushions betrayed her. Her balance lost, she slid gently down the little hill until her soft hip ran into his steel frame.

'Hey, tears?' One of his arms came around her shoulders and bonded her to him.

'Don't be silly,' she sobbed. 'I *never* cry.'

'Yes, I can see that. Try my handkerchief. It's bigger than yours. For a girl who's not crying, you do a good job of it.'

'Don't you patronise me!' she roared at him. 'Don't you ever——'

'Who, me?' He took an extra tuck with his arm, and her head, unable to reach his shoulder, ended up against his chest. 'Whatever I shouldn't, I don't, believe me.'

'I'm only doing this because I'm tired,' she stated firmly, and then had another idea. 'Dealing with your daughter was emotionally wearing. I was exhausted *before* you dragged me off to that dumb dinner. And it's all your fault!'

'Of course it is,' he said soothingly. 'Whatever—it's all my fault. And I *do* appreciate what you've done for my daughter. And me, for that matter. I would have looked very strange sitting up there on the dais without my fiancée. And now it's over?'

She sneaked a peek at him. He actually *looked* as if he disliked the ending. Strange. His big eyes seemed to be bigger, deeper than ever. There was a spark of—regret in them. Stiffen your spine, she commanded herself. Stiff upper lip. Whatever!

'And now it's over,' she confirmed, sniffing back the tears and doing her best to establish some personal space between them. That was the moment that Mabel Baines returned, pushing a wheeled trolley loaded with drinks and sandwiches.

The tall, gaunt housekeeper measured the attitude in the room as she wheeled the trolley into position. And had the common sense to say nothing about tears or passions or wet handkerchiefs. 'Ham salad,' she announced. 'Or sliced turkey, if you prefer. And hot tea.'

'I prefer coffee,' he grumbled.

'No coffee,' the housekeeper reprimanded. 'It keeps you awake at night. Always did. Drink the tea.'

'Yes, ma'am,' he quipped. 'You see,' he said mournfully to Valeria, 'that's what happens when your housekeeper used to change your nappies. There's no end to the things they remember about you.'

'True,' Mabel said caustically. 'Including what a nasty boy you really were in those days. Now, love, what's the matter?'

'Nothing,' Val insisted as she struggled to her feet. 'I—got something in my eye.'

'Yes, I can see you did,' Mrs Baines said sarcastically. 'Something about the size of an engagement ring? Bart Thomas, you really are the most!'

'Hey, I'm as innocent as the driven snow,' he objected. 'I was just standing here with a stupid smile on my face, and she handed back my ring. Not *my* idea at all!'

'The whole thing was *your* idea.' Valeria was still struggling with the quiet tears. His handkerchief was soaked—and besides, it was *his*. She was about to open the flood-gates and really lay him out when the telephone rang.

'I'll get it,' he said. 'Mabel, see if you can turn off the waterfall.'

He was one of those men who was lazy about small details. Not for him the need to hold a telephone in hand,

tied to one place by the length of the cord. His telephones were all speakerphones. One merely pressed a
button, and the conversations on both ends could be
heard through the amplifier. 'Thomas here,' he said. The
telephone squawked at him until he adjusted the volume
control.

'Malcom Graves,' the voice at the other end said.

'The governor's principal secretary,' Bart told the two
women softly.

'Did you hear the eleven o'clock news, Mr Thomas?'

'No, I didn't. I was out at a local banquet. Something
important?'

'Something very important,' Graves said. 'The
governor is concerned. Switch on channel seven. They
might still be running the item.'

Mabel was already at the television set, but they were
a moment too late for the full article. 'And so the senator
will be raising a point of order in the legislature
tomorrow,' the station anchorwoman was saying, 'con-
cerning the morality of *some* of the governor's nomi-
nees to the Bench. Now this word from——'

Mabel snapped the switch off. Bart shook his head in
disgust as he moved closer to the telephone. 'Which
senator?'

'Who else?' Graves said. 'Senator Poitras. He's an
idiot, but we're on shaky ground already, nominating a
divorced man. You can say what you want to about
liberal politics, but the Commonwealth is still mainly
Catholic, mainly conservative in its feelings about family
life.'

'I—don't think Senator Poitras can stand the heat,'
Bart said cautiously. 'Maybe we have someone who could
pass the word to him gently?'

'How gently?' Graves asked impatiently. 'About
what?'

'About his daughter Amelé,' Bart answered. 'She's the one who is blowing the whistle, and she can't stand the light of day on *her* activities. I threw her out of my house and she must have gone straight to Daddy to blow the whistle. If the senator wants to play hardball, I'd be glad to make a statement about my relationship with his daughter. To the Press, of course. Maybe you could have someone tell him about that before he gets up in the Senate tomorrow?'

'That's terrible,' Graves laughed. 'That's blackmail, Mr Thomas. I think I just might call the great man myself. Amelé, that's the girl's name? Then who is this other one? The contention is that you're living with someone by the name of Valeria down there.'

'Oh, you mean my fiancée, Valeria Brewster,' Bart chuckled. 'A real old family name in the Commonwealth. A lovely woman. A schoolteacher. Yes, she's living in my house, serving as a companion to my daughter. And we have a chaperon in residence as well.'

Why, he sounds so sincere I could almost believe it myself, Val thought. How can a man be so smooth and silky when all the time he's lying? I ought to——

'Brewster,' Graves murmured. 'Nice name. Good recognition value. Not bad. Hang on to her, and maybe we can ride out the storm. Folks accept a lot under the title of fiancée these days. Or make it even better—marry the girl.'

'Yes,' Bart returned gently. 'We intend to. In just a couple of weeks.'

'Well, I won't upset the governor tonight,' Graves said genially. 'The hearings will start next week some time. Just keep out of trouble until then. The gov counts on you.' There was no goodbye. The sound of the dial tone resounded through the room.

'Well, now,' Mrs Baines said, 'You two get busy on the eats. I think I'll go back to the kitchen and——' She didn't finish the statement because nobody was paying attention. Valeria was standing in front of the fireplace, hands on hips, a slow boil building up inside her as she stared at Bart Thomas, who was doing his best to appear Mr Innocence.

'Well,' Valeria said in absolute disgust, 'you've done it again, haven't you?'

'I do believe I have,' he offered apologetically. He moved over in front of her, a hang-dog look on his face, his hand extended toward her. Between his big thumb and forefinger the ring. 'Please.'

'And now it's worse than before,' she muttered angrily. 'Now you have to add on that bit about marriage! My God!'

'As you say,' he murmured softly.

There were a million things she wanted to say, a thousand vases she wanted to throw at him, a hundred hurts she wanted to inflicted on his superior frame, a decade of insults about his parentage—and one thought. I need—that ring, she told herself. Not him! God, no, not him, but that ring. It's *my* name they'll have in the Boston papers tomorrow. I'd sink right through the earth if the parishioners at Gran's church heard about it without the 'engagement' to paper it over. Of *course* I don't need him. And of *course* there isn't going to be a wedding!

And all the while the little voice of her conscience battered at her. The ring doesn't mean a thing to you, Valeria Brewster, and you know it. Once you've told yourself *one* lie, how easy it is to tell another—and another!

'Shut up,' Val muttered. She extended her own left hand, and the ring slipped back into the little groove it had developed over the past weeks. Valeria Brewster sighed a gusty sigh of relief, and held it up to the light.

'But no wedding,' she insisted. His eyes flared wider, but he said nothing. 'And *you* get to tell your daughter,' she continued, licking her lips nervously.

'Coward,' he chuckled. 'Thank you.' And then he kissed her.

There was nothing warm and comforting about *this* kiss. It sparked off a riot from the moment of impact, sending flurries of excitement racing up and down her spine. It demanded something of her, and, unpractised, she did her best in return, standing on tiptoes, with both hands barely able to reach around his neck.

The clock on the mantel sounded midnight, and got no attention at all. Five minutes later, when Mabel Baines popped back into the room, Valeria was moaning and squirming, trying her best to get closer to him.

'Well, I see it's *already* been fixed,' the housekeeper said as she gently closed the door behind her and walked back to the kitchen.

# CHAPTER SEVEN

THE HOUSE was very quiet at seven in the morning, even though the sun had been up for an hour. A pair of jays were making raucous noises outside the living-room window, and a breeze rattled the branches of the old oak tree that stood closest to the building.

'Another two weeks till school starts,' Valeria reminded herself as she sipped at her mug of instant coffee and studied yesterday's *Boston Globe*. There was no foolishness about Valeria Brewster this morning; she was dressed for action. A pair of faded jeans, a long-sleeved blouse, her hair braided to be out of the way, and not a touch of make-up.

It would be an outdoor day, and there was a threat of rain for the late afternoon. Another two weeks, she thought. Back to my little house by the pond; the end of a delightful summer story. Goodbye to Maria and Maria's father. For some reason, she couldn't bring herself to even think the man's name. Such thoughts brought strange feelings. She held up her left hand and admired his ring again, just as she had done late last night.

'But there *won't* be a wedding,' she muttered.

Maria came in at just that moment. A sober, bitter Maria, with an intelligence beyond her years. 'Just keep saying that,' the girl said sarcastically. 'Say it ten times over, four times a day, and maybe somebody will believe you.'

'I take it you don't,' Valeria asked glumly. 'I thought your father was going to explain it all to you.'

Rudolph, who had collapsed across Val's feet, wagged his tail a couple of times, thumping the floor, but made not a move. 'And I don't think your dog does, either,' the child responded as she walked jauntily over to the chair opposite Val and sat down.

Maria's face bore the ravages of her grief and anger, but the tears had dried up and had been replaced by a look of—cunning. That was the only word that Val could search out that fitted. The child was plotting *something*. And when a youthful Borgia plotted, it would do well for elderly schoolteachers to tread warily, Valeria told herself. Perhaps a change of direction?

'It's hard to tell what Rudy's thinking,' she said gently. 'When I was your age he would run and romp and play with me for hours, but now he can hardly keep going. The poor old guy has arthritis in all his legs, and I think his eyesight is fading.'

'Then you ought to have him put down,' Maria said. 'He's not doing anyone any good like that.'

Val sat up a little in her chair. Callousness, she had not expected. 'I wouldn't do that,' she replied fiercely. 'He's earned his rest and dignity. Lord, if we put down everyone who's gone past his prime, this town would be de-populated. How about you? Are you useful? Maybe we ought to put *you* down.'

'Why not?' the girl snapped. 'I might be better off.' And then suddenly a mask came down over her face, just as if she had deliberately lowered a curtain. 'You really aren't going to marry my father?'

'I really am not,' Valeria said flatly. And then, loud enough to be heard down the hall, *'I really am not going to marry your father!'*

'No use shouting the house down.' Maria managed a half-smile, her first in some days. 'Papa went to Boston early this morning.'

'Did he really?' Valeria, who had been awake half the night, found it hard to believe that he had left without her knowing it. But that certainly made things easier in the short term.

'He came to my room before he left,' the girl continued, again with that half-smile on her face. 'You getting married, and him getting to be a judge, that's all mixed up together, isn't it?'

'In a way.' Val checked her watch. The bus would be by to pick her up in thirty minutes. Her coffee was cold, but she sipped at it anyway.

'And if he didn't get to be a judge, you wouldn't have to get married?'

'Look, I don't know what you're going on about.' Val leaned forward in her chair and tried to read the girl's face, as she often did in her classes. But this child was a master of disguise. She looked altogether bland and innocent—two characteristics that, any teacher knew, never mix in a teenager. 'Your father has this bug in his ear about being a judge. That I know. *He* seems to think that if we marry, he and I, it will help him to the appointment.'

'And what do you think?'

'I don't know whether it will or not, Maria. But I haven't any mad urge to be married to a judge—or to your father, for that matter. So maybe you're right. If he didn't get to sit on the Bench, perhaps he wouldn't be spouting off about marriage!'

'Ah!' the girl settled back, a scheming look back on her face. Val nibbled at her toast, finished off her coffee, and weighed the silence.

'So, what are you up to today?' All innocence, that question. Perhaps she's got off the marry-my-father carousel, Val thought. Walk carefully!

'Nothing much,' she said. 'I had a call earlier from a group of—concerned people with whom I sometimes co-operate. They're gathering a small crowd to—make a public statement down on the Cape.'

Maria's face lit up. 'You're gonna picket someplace!'

'Well, in a manner of speaking,' Val replied. 'There was a big incident down at Camp Edwards yesterday. It's all in the paper there.' Maria snatched up the newspaper and scanned the headlines.

'Wow, a real artillery shell?'

'As it says. The National Guard was practising with their artillery, and some group of them managed to land a shell completely off the reservation, right in the middle of Route Six. Luckily nobody was driving down the road at the moment, but that's one of the busiest highways in the whole area.'

'That's a silly place to shoot cannons.'

'Years ago, when they established the camp, it made sense, dear. That whole area was a sort of dead end. Now there are towns growing up all around it, and they still use it for artillery practice—and a lot of other things. So a group of us will conduct a small demonstration at the gates to the camp.' And just why, pray tell me, are you interested in such goings on, Maria Thomas? Val asked herself. And was unable to provide an answer. She frowned thoughtfully.

'Oh, keen,' the girl chuckled. 'I wanna come with you.'

Valeria looked over the table. The girl wore a big smile, appeared anxious to help, but her eyes were hard as steel. A danger signal went up in Val's mind. 'No, you can't come with us,' she told the child. 'It's no place for someone your age. This is a passive demonstration. Children lose their tempers too easily. And that could lead to all of us ending up in jail. No, I don't think so.'

'I don't *look* like a child,' Maria persisted. 'I bet that no fuzz could tell how old I am.' She straightened up and took a deep breath, throwing her breasts into stark outline against her blouse.

'It isn't your figure I worry about,' Val insisted, 'it's your mind. Just what are you up to, young lady?'

'I'm up to going out with you and helping. This is a good cause, and I have to learn to be a protester. You can teach me, or else——'

'Ah. Now we come to the "or else". Or else what, miss?'

'Or else I'm going to tell Papa all about you and your protests. Everything!'

And there's the sword behind the toreador's cape, Val said, biting her lower lip. Thirteen years old, and an accomplished blackmailer. This one will go a long way! 'Maybe I wouldn't care if you told him,' she tried cautiously.

'And maybe you would,' the child responded. In that moment she appeared to be a woman a thousand years old. 'I've watched you, you know. You don't fool me much.'

'Oh, really?' And what a stupid gambit *that* is, Val thought. How weak can you get, Miss Brewster?

'Well, I know a way to find out,' Maria said as she bounced to her feet. 'You just go ahead without me, and I'll start writing it all out so I'll have it straight when my father gets home.'

And you really will, won't you? Val asked herself as she struggled to come to a better conclusion than the obvious one. But the secret to high-class blackmailing is to leave your victim no way to wiggle, and this little girl was one of the best. Luckily I don't give a darn if her father knows about my work or not! Is that so? her conscience asked in all syrupy sweetness. Yes, that's so,

Valeria snapped, and then recognised the truth. Of course I care!

'All right,' Valeria sighed. 'Get yourself dressed in something durable and demure. Especially check your shoes. It's hard work, walking a picket line in the sun. And a hat or something to wear. When we get there, for Pete's sake, watch yourself. Keep calm. There's more than one busted head come out of a passive demonstration!'

'Busted head?' the girl repeated sarcastically. 'And you a schoolteacher? What grammar!'

'It's hard to speak properly to a blackmailer,' Val returned angrily. Maria had the grace to blush.

The two women returned to the house just in front of the thunderstorm, dashing up the front steps to avoid getting soaked. Mrs Baines held the door for them.

'Four o'clock,' the housekeeper grumbled. 'Somebody could have told me where they went, you know. All that lunch spoiled. Did you get anything to eat today?'

'No,' Val admitted cautiously. 'We—found ourselves too busy to get a bite.'

'Hmmph,' the housekeeper snorted. 'Foolishness. Go sit in the living-room and I'll bring you some tea and cakes.'

'Coffee,' Valeria interjected. 'I can't stand tea.'

'Milk,' Maria asked. 'I can't stand coffee.'

'Humph,' Mrs Baines commented. 'Mr Thomas isn't back from Boston yet, either. Nor Harry. Crazy household. Only me and the dog, all day, and the lord only knows which one of us is the worse off.' Still muttering, she took herself off in the general direction of the kitchen.

'We didn't make a hit there,' Val commented as she led the way down the hall.

'I wouldn't say that.' Maria, face flushed from having spent almost a full day in sun and wind, was smiling broadly. 'In all the time I've known Mrs Baines, you're the first one she ever offered to feed except at meal time. Even Papa has to forage for himself.'

'I don't know why I would rate *that* high.' Valeria unbuttoned the top two buttons of her blouse, now that she was out of the wind. The rain smashed against the window-panes, and thunder rolled. Rudolph came galloping down the hall, arthritis and all, his claws rattling for purchase on the highly polished floor.

'My dog hates thunderstorms,' Val explained indulgently as the old animal stretched out over her feet.

'Me, too,' Maria quipped. 'Look at that rain. We're lucky we didn't drown out there. It was fun!'

'It wasn't meant to be fun,' Val reprimanded. 'Your little argument with those men brought us to within a stone's throw of a riot, girl. If you intend to be a useful demonstrator you must learn not to react to anything that's said by others outside the group! People get hurt in riots. Some very badly.'

'I didn't do anything on purpose,' Maria groused. That thoughtful look was back on her face again.

'It doesn't matter *why* you did it,' Valeria persisted. 'Our goal was to get a friendly response from the media. We were doing fine until that little altercation blew up. Luckily the cameras were tracking the sheriff at that moment. Otherwise your face would be all over the evening TV news!'

'Would it really?' And there were those little wheels revolving in the girl's head again, so plainly that Valeria could see them. But not plainly enough to reveal the cause.

'Yes, really,' Val added. 'And *that* would really put the cat among the pigeons. Not to mention what it might

do to your father's nomination. Can you see the headlines? ''Judicial nominee's daughter arrested for insti-
gating riot!'' Wouldn't that be a great story?'

'Well, I suppose we won't have to wait for ever,' Maria
sighed. 'The governor's council will have their vote pretty
soon, and then it won't matter, will it? Papa will be a
judge, and you will——'

'There isn't going to be any marriage,' Valeria said
firmly. 'Get it through your little head—I am not going
to marry your father!'

'Bravely said!' The deep, melodious voice sounded
right at Val's ear. She whipped around in her chair and
glared at him.

'Don't *do* that,' she protested. 'You take ten years off
my life every time you sneak up on me!'

'Papa,' Maria acknowledged, skittering up off her
chair and backing away in a completely uncharacteristic
manner.

'Don't everybody be so enthusiastic about welcoming
me home,' he said dolefully. 'Should I carry a little bell
to ring, and go around crying *''Unclean, Unclean''*?'

'You are undoubtedly one of the biggest hams in the
law business,' Val groaned. 'Spare me any more. Maria
and I were—Maria? Where the devil did she go?'

'Slipped off into the wild blue yonder,' he chuckled.
'But still, seeing her out of her room is pure profit,
Valeria. You have a way with children.'

'Don't start that stuff,' Val insisted. 'I haven't any
idea why she came out of *purdah*. I haven't the slightest
idea how, or what that girl thinks about. All I know is
that she's up to something!'

'Up to something?' He walked over to confront her.
'As in *trouble*?'

'As in trouble,' she sighed. 'With a capital T. And
you might notice that I'm not all that pleased with you,

either, Mr Thomas.' She had been practising her glare all day, but the outdoor exercise on the picket line had worn her out. Rated on a scale of one to ten, this particular glare hardly rated a five. And he was no help at all. He stood there, contemplating, looking tired himself, and so darn—boyish—that it ate at her heart!

'Why don't we have a drink to relax us?' he offered, moving over to the sideboard, 'and then we'll have dinner. What's Mabel working on tonight?'

'Fish,' she told him disgustedly. 'What else? It's Friday. Some sort of trout thing.'

'You don't like fish?'

'That's about the kindest thing you could say about it,' she muttered. And now you're going to tell me it's good for my health, and every grown woman should eat it at least twice a week. And liver on the alternate day, right? she thought. Just exactly what Gran always said before she tried to stuff it down my throat. And I don't intend to eat it for you, Mr Bart Thomas, any more than I ate it for Gran! So take that!

He seemed marvellously unaffected by her internal struggle, but handed her a glass of liquid encouragement. 'Whisky Sour,' he identified the mix. She tasted.

It had the sweet tang about it of cold lemonade, with a bite behind the lemon. But since it was so obviously only a fruit drink, she tossed it off over his protest. And when he offered his arm she took it in the grand manner. They paraded down the hall to the dining-room just as Mabel Baines sounded the dinner bell, and at the table, without a demur, she ate—fish!

'I've got a TV programme I have to watch tonight,' Maria said as soon as the dessert had been gulped. The child's eyes were narrowed as she watched both Val and her father. Danger signals reverberated through Val's head. Get them separated, she shouted at herself. But there was some semblance of teaching required of her job.

'You've also got six pages of maths to do,' she announced, and almost bit her tongue as Maria smiled at her.

'Yes,' the child admitted. 'Instead of doing schoolwork, we went out today, Papa.'

'That must have been exciting.' He looked like a man doing his duty to his only child. If Maria had said they were out all afternoon modelling in the nude he probably would have said 'That's nice.'

'Don't you want to know what we did?' Maria moved back into her chair and sniffed at Val, as if challenging her to interrupt.

'Yes, of course,' her father answered.

'Well, we went down the Cape, to Camp Edwards, and we joined a bunch of other people there and picketed the front gate and raised a fuss about the artillery firing.'

'And nobody wore any clothes and the policemen assassinated the President,' Valeria added, giving Maria a cool, calm look.

'That's nice,' Bart said absent-mindedly. 'I'm glad you had a good time. I need to talk to you, Valeria.'

'Papa!' the girl yelled, and when he looked rather vacantly at her she shrugged her shoulders and muttered something that sounded like, 'Oh, well.' She managed one more nasty look in Valeria's direction, and ran out of the room.

'Now what was *that* all about?' Bart asked. Valeria, who had both elbows on the table, resting her chin in the cup of her hands, managed a shrug of the shoulders and a lifted eyebrow. Bart Thomas was beginning to react to stimuli much as her grandfather had. She had made a detailed study of her grandfather the judge, and immediately felt herself to be on more secure ground.

'Who knows what goes on in adolescent minds?' she murmured. 'And you have no idea how much I need to talk to you, Mr Thomas.'

Mabel, who had chosen not to share the meal, bustled in just at that moment. 'Can we have coffee on the back terrace?' he asked.

'Irish?' Mabel pursued her lips. The housekeepers forebears came from Germany, but she held a great affection for Irish libations, a distinct contradiction to her normally Puritan beliefs.

'Not for me,' Valeria interjected. The fruit drink had left her feeling somewhat confused. Her fatigue, banished for a moment by the dinner conversation, had returned four-fold, and she had no intention at all of being less than attentive when the 'talk' began. It was bad enough that the back terrace was segregated from the rest of the house, and a full moon was coming up out of the ocean. A girl could hardly afford too many strikes on her—and the subject was serious! 'Just black coffee.'

'One black, one Irish,' he confirmed.

'Mabel,' she asked, curious, as Mrs Baines winked an eye at him and turned to leave. 'How come you didn't have dinner with the rest of us tonight?'

'Oh, no reason in particular,' the housekeeper chuckled. 'It's just that Harry and I can't stand fish. We had burgers and chips in the kitchen.'

'Well, I'll be——'

'Come on,' he told her as he rose to help with her chair. It was hard *not* to come on. He took possession of her arm and marched her smartly back down the hall and out on to the terrace. In the doing she lost a shoe, but he was so intent on his purpose that he hardly noticed her hobbling movement.

The moon *was* up, perched just on the ocean's curve, establishing a fairy path of silvery beams. She jerked to a stop half-way through the french windows of the living-room. 'You did that on purpose,' she muttered. Her ordered life seemed to be falling into little tiny pieces.

'The chairs?' He walked over to the two loungers and rattled one of them to see if there were a problem. 'Harry put these out here yesterday.'

'I *don't* mean the darn chairs,' she said flatly. But it would sound so absolutely stupid to say 'the moonlight' that she bit her tongue and strangled the words a-borning.

'Oh, you mean the set-up—chairs, table, bug-light? We always have that arrangement. It's just you've been so busy with your writing and pamphleteering, you've not seen it. Sit down over here. As soon as I get this thing going the bugs will disappear completely.'

'Yes, of course,' she sighed, and followed him out, limping.

'You hurt your foot?'

No, she told herself, but if I'm not careful I'm liable to hurt a lot more than a foot. Where the devil is that coffee?

'Somebody left a shoe in the hall,' Mabel interrupted, as she wheeled out a coffee-tray. 'Maria's, maybe. That girl has bigger feet than I do. I'll just leave the coffee-makings here, and get the kitchen cleaned up.'

Valeria sank carefully into the lounge chair. My God, see what's come over you, she lectured herself sternly, doing her best to hide her face from Bart's view. First you learn to tell lies, and you begin to live the lies, and now you haven't even the gumption to admit that you lost *your* shoe. Poor Maria. I wonder how many other people's sins she suffers from!

'Don't hide from me,' Bart complained. 'This is an important conversation. I hate to have my witnesses out of sight during the interrogation.'

'I'm not a courtroom witness.' She managed to shape her voice into a calm, cool schoolteacher's weapon. It was a difficult job, and took a lot of doing. 'I'm only unbraiding my hair,' she added. 'I've worn it this way all day, and it's just a little bit tight. You wouldn't know about things like that!'

'No,' he laughed. 'I don't think I've had my hair in braids since—oh, since I was six months old. Sugar and milk?'

'Black,' she insisted. And hurry, man. Black coffee, before my mouth runs away with me. The bottom of the mug almost burned her hand as he poured and passed it over. She yelped and shifted her grip.

'What?' He leaned over her in the dusk, a huge, dark shadow, both promising and threatening. Keeping ahead of him, juggling all her various concealed plots in her head, was giving her a headache. Valeria leaned back in her chair and sipped.

'I saw the governor for lunch.' He dropped the announcement casually in front of her. Valeria, who had seen the governor of the Commonwealth once—on television—sat up straight in her chair, took a deeper draught of the coffee, and came up sputtering. 'Hey, it wasn't all *that* important,' he chuckled as he pounded on her back.

'Don't——' she gasped for breath. 'Don't break my back!'

'Hey, I thought I was helping,' he replied mournfully. The hand that had been pounding her between her shoulder-blades, shifted up across her cheek in a soft caress.

'Don't!' she managed in a half-whisper. Any sort of contact with him seemed dangerous—it *had* to be the moonlight! She shifted away from him and then relaxed in the chair and stared out along the moon-path toward the harbour. Darkness had sent the gulls to cover; human noises were muted at the dinner hour. Only the splash of waves, and the rustling of small life in the oak branches could be heard. And the odours—the sharp sea smell mixed with the perfume of flowering ramblers—and just a touch of the coffee smell from the pot between them—all had a heady effect.

I'm only his daughter's companion, she argued beneath her breath. He's only a man with a business connection. A large, good-looking man, but only a business connection, nevertheless. Get a hold on your nerves, Valeria Brewster! And remember, lawyers and used-car salesmen rank very close to the bottom of the 'dependable people' list!

'You're not interested in what the governor and I did?' he prodded.

'Why—you said you had lunch,' she returned. Her voice had risen slightly, moving dangerously in the direction of hysteria. She smothered it, and tried again. 'I suppose you went to the Hilton and were nude?'

'I heard what you said at the dinner table,' he chuckled. In the darkness his bulk shifted, as if he were leaning in her direction. His chair scraped. Valeria felt a sort of claustrophobia engulfing her. 'No, we weren't nude. Yes, we had a drink or two. No, there weren't any dancing girls. But——'

'I don't think I want to hear any *buts*,' she said primly.

'Dammit, Valeria Brewster,' he growled, 'you're going to hear them. The Governor tells me that the vote in the council will be soon—within a few days. He also tells me that the politicians on the council are sitting on the fence, willing to jump either way. Although we got Senator Poitras to suspend his little war, his daughter is spreading gossip all over Boston. Evidently Amelé went straight from Plymouth to a columnist she knows in Beantown.'

'Well, that's terrible,' Valeria managed to squeak. 'But then—you shouldn't go out with that kind of girl!'

'That kind of girl has suited me very well in the past,' he said stiffly. She could feel the tension rising again as she considered what he had said. Which was the important part? 'Suited me very well'? Or the other—'in the past'? 'Suit me' in what way? Luckily there were speckles of cloud that blurred the moon for a moment or two, or he would have seen the blush that spread all the way up to the roots of her hair.

'Yes,' she sighed. 'It's none of my business, is it?'

'Wrong again, Valeria. It's certainly *is* your business.'

She ducked her head, letting her heavy, dark hair swing forward around her face. I don't *want* him to explain, she told herself. I don't want him to!

'I've never known a woman like you,' he continued. His voice was caressingly soft, incredibly compelling.

'Not fair,' she murmured softly. 'I *know* it's been a long time since you were in high school, but you must have had *some* female teachers!'

'That's not what I mean!' His chair scraped again as he moved closer. 'You know damn well that's not what I mean!'

Anger pulsed at her out of the darkness. She sat up, swung her feet down to the bricks of the terrace, and pushed herself up to a standing position. 'I *don't* know,' she insisted through clenched teeth. 'I don't *want* to know. And I don't have to sit here and be insulted. I'm an employee, not a whipping boy!'

The moon did not provide enough light. The room behind them was dark. A terrible excitement closed in on her as his dark bulk came closer. She wanted—she didn't know *what* she wanted. Desires were overwhelmed by fears. If she gave him one little inch he would sweep her away in a torrent of passion, and that she could not accept. Valeria summoned up anger to help in the contest.

'Don't do that,' she muttered as she took a step away from him. Too late. His hands were on her shoulders, halting her movement but not pulling her in his direction. Fixed, she trembled so much that he could feel the shaking.

'I'm not doing anything—yet,' he exclaimed softly. 'And if I did, you'd like it.' His voice had sunk to that level that was soft seduction, but all it did was increase her fears.

'Not on your life,' she snapped, pulling herself up out of her fantasies. 'Turn me loose, Mr Thomas. Now!'

'Threats?' he crowed softly. 'We're going to be married, Valeria. You and I——'

'Why do I have to keep telling you?' she cried softly. 'I—am—not—going—to—marry—you! Watch my lips. I'll say it again!'

'Don't bother,' he sighed, and the sound seemed to come from his heart in a gusty rush. He manoeuvred her back to her lounge chair, and removed his hands. 'Sit down, Valeria—please?'

It might have been the 'please'. She sank into the chair as if someone had unfastened the locks on her knees. Flustered, out of breath, as if she had jogged five miles in those tense minutes, she collapsed against the back of the chair and pulled her legs up. Count to ten. Do it again! His figure bulked in the darkness, farther away, as he sat gingerly on the edge of his own chair and watched her. Count to ten more, she commanded herself. Gradually her pulse slowed, her breath came more easily.

'Let's keep it on a business basis,' his deep voice commented. 'All I'm asking is an extension of what we've been doing for a week or more.'

'Ten days,' she interjected quietly. 'Ten days of lying to people.'

He cleared his throat. 'Nobody's hurt by it. White lies are not all that damning. I'm in a fix. You know how much I want this seat on the Bench. Maybe we don't have to get married, Valeria. Maybe all we have to do is act like we're *going* to get married. If the council vote comes soon—that could be all that's necessary. If not—well——'

'Yes,' she snapped. 'That's the interesting part. If not, well what?'

'There's nothing all that permanent about marriage,' he muttered. 'Almost forty per cent of all marriages don't work. If we *have* to get married, we can have it annulled as soon as the council has voted.'

'And in the meantime?' It was hard for her to keep the shrill fear out of her voice. He heard it, and chuckled in the dark.

'And in the meantime, nothing,' he returned gently. 'It will be entirely platonic, my dear.' Almost, she could lead herself to believe he sighed again. She clung desperately to the thought. 'After all,' he continued, 'you're not exactly my kind of girl, Miss Brewster!'

He might just as well have stabbed her with a dull knife. The pain sliced through to her heart. Amelé, that was *his* type. Curvaceous, sophisticated, available! All the things she could not be. Nor could she understand why it hurt so much to face the fact. Her head ached suddenly. She ran her fingers through her hair and then pressed them against her temple. She was a logical and pragmatic woman. Surely there must be some—straight path back to normality?

'I don't like it,' she said finally. 'You're making some sort of a game out of a holy ceremony. I—just don't like it. Yes, I've heard you say time after time that you'd kill to get this appointment. But that has nothing to do with me. You must see that. I might be willing to—play along with some small part of your crazy scenario, but you're going to have to do some tall talking to convince me that there's not a need for it. Just *why* do you have to be a judge? Just because your father——'

He was up on his feet before she could finish. 'You don't know a single thing about—my father,' he rasped. The temperature in their immediate vicinity dropped ten degrees or more as he paced back and forth. Three steps one way, three the other. A quick stalking, as he made up his mind.

He came to a stop directly in front of her. 'So all right, I haven't been *completely* honest with you. And I wouldn't—except that I need your help so very much. And let me tell you something——' he reached down and tapped a finger on her aching forehead '—if any of *this* gets out, I've blown every last chance I'll ever have to get an appointment. If you whisper this to your Mrs Herlihy——'

'I don't go around peddling secrets,' she interrupted, growling at him. 'And she's not *my* Mrs Herlihy. If this thing is all that important, don't tell me. I'm not asking for any confidences!'

'The hell you're not,' he snapped, rocking back and forth on the balls of his feet. Thinking, Val told herself. He had started to talk, and then realised how foolish it would be to share something, and now he's thinking. Well, he can think until—that place—freezes over, for all of me. I don't *want* to hear! She covered her ears with her hands.

'Don't tell me,' she begged. 'Just don't tell me.'

He stooped beside her chair, so his head was level with her own. 'You don't leave me any choice,' he stated flatly. 'You're the only woman in the world who can help me now. And I *need* your help.'

Even though I'm not your type, she thought. Unbidden, her hand moved to touch his cheek. It was rough, warm. He needs to shave twice a day. The inconsequential thought ran through her mind and relieved some of her tension. The headache disappeared as fast as it had come.

'My father is dead,' he said slowly. He seemed to be searching for words, groping in the dark. 'He died in Huntsville, Texas.' There was a pause, as if he expected her to know the town, to say something.

'But I——' She fumbled for something to say, but the name was totally unfamiliar, and you could hardly say 'That's nice,' when a man suddenly announces that his father is dead!

'Huntsville, Texas,' he repeated. 'The biggest prison in the state of Texas.' The words seemed to boom on the quiet air, floating there, echoing.

'Your father died in prison?' she gasped.

'Yes,' he said gloomily. 'Years ago. He was an immigrant, with no great command of the language, and got involved in a riot. They sentenced him to life.'

'Life for rioting?' She choked on the words. 'They—nobody—did he kill somebody?'

'No, he didn't kill somebody.' His words seemed suddenly remote, as if he were a long distance away, shouting down the wrong end of a megaphone. 'And yes, they sentenced him to life. They didn't know, but they sentenced him to life. Three to five years was the way the judge put it. My father died in two, of cancer. They wouldn't even let him come home to be with his family when he was dying! The judge on the original case refused to review the ameliorating evidence.'

'Oh, God,' she said, her agony overflowing.

'Yes—oh, God,' he repeated. 'When I saw him last I was just sixteen. He told me many things. And exacted a promise. "It's a great, good country," he told me. "But everything is so big, and sometimes people become so little that accidents happen. Promise me, son, that you'll grow up and help make some small improvement in the legal system."'

The clouds cleared the face of the moon at just that moment. Valeria could see the twisted pain written across his brow in the silver light, and it tugged at her heart again.

'And so,' he continued matter-of-factly, 'I went into law, and now I've come to the conclusion that the only way I can keep my promise is by sitting on the Bench myself.'

Her hand reached out for him as her heart did, but he was up and pacing before she could touch him. For minutes he paced, and then he came back to her again.

'So there you have my reason,' he commented coolly. 'It may not seem much to you, but promises are important—at least, I think so. I need your help to keep this promise. Will you?'

Oh, God she sighed to herself. Promises *are* important. Of course they are. And with all that pain, he has these other things to worry him. But—marriage is for ever. He can talk blithely about annulments and divorces, but *I* can't. I'd have to be very much in love with a man before I'd agree to *marry* him!

'Well,' she said cautiously, tasting every word before she released it, 'I don't mind going through the motions.

Making the arrangements, talking it over—that sort of thing. But you'd better hurry the council vote, because—there's no way I could actually marry you, Mr Thomas. And I have to leave it in your hands to explain to your daughter what we're about. Your last explanation about our engagement didn't go over very well with her!'

His tall figure seemed to relax. In the moonlight it was hard to tell. Which is one of the troubles with moonlight, she lectured herself severely. It's almost impossible to see clearly in matters of the heart!

'Well——' he paused. 'If that's what's on offer, I gladly accept. I'll take care of Maria. And I'm going to increase your pay by ten per cent.'

'No!' She was on her feet without realising it. 'No! You can't *pay* a woman money to do something like this!'

'Of course you're right,' he laughed. 'But there ought to be *some* payment.'

There was something. A delightful payment, and he knew exactly how to make it. Warmth and arms and moonlight all encompassed Valeria, squeezing the logic entirely out of her tired mind. But pragmatism was something else. It clung to its disciples through thick and thin.

If kissing is inevitable, she heard her conscience nag at her, lie back and enjoy it!

# CHAPTER EIGHT

MONDAY morning brought showers streaming across Plymouth on a south-easterly wind. The temperature dropped dramatically, down to a shivery sixty-five degrees, with tempers to match.

'You're going to Boston again?' Valeria asked at the breakfast table. She was dressed for another working day, despite the weather. Her lovely red hair was pinned up in a coronet, her denims were aged to a homey grey, and her simple white blouse was of indestructible nylon. He was wearing a dark blue suit and a frown.

'Any reason why I shouldn't?'

'Well, I—no,' she admitted, turning back to her oatmeal. 'I thought I would—you know—make a gesture about the wedding, and to be sure we're singing off the same page of music, I——'

'Get to the point,' he grumbled as he reached for the morning paper. 'I don't have all day.'

'And of course I do,' she replied sarcastically. 'This is like playing Romeo and Juliet with a broomstick for Romeo!' She slammed her spoon down on the table. 'Did you tell your daughter?'

'Don't nag me before I've had my coffee!' He folded the newspaper and laid it down carefully beside his plate before he looked across the table at her. 'Yes, I told my daughter.'

Valeria could see the uneasy expression that flashed across his face before he turned away to look out the window. Somehow she knew. He wouldn't deliberately lie, so that raised the question: just what *did* he tell Maria? The whole truth or, like the spate of advertising on the value of aloe in soap, was there only enough truth to make it legal to use the word on the label? She drummed her fingers on the table for a moment, and then picked up her spoon and went back to the cooling oatmeal.

'So have your coffee,' she snapped. 'Because you're not getting out of this house until we have some agreement.'

'For a woman who hasn't even got the job yet, you've turned into a bossy wife,' he grunted as he snatched up his mug and sipped.

'You'll remember I never asked for the job, as you call it,' she argued, 'and you haven't seen *bossy*—yet! Now, there's no way I want to involve a minister and a church in this charade.'

'Of course not.' He took another sip, and grounded the mug angrily. 'God, why can't I even get hot coffee for breakfast? Everything's going to pot in this house!'

'Try pouring some from the hot pot,' she pointed out sarcastically, 'and stop dodging the problem.'

He cocked one eye at her, and reached over for the electric coffee-pot at his elbow. 'Say, you are in a bad temper, aren't you?' he commented.

'You haven't seen *bad* yet, either,' she said determinedly. Her pointed little chin was up in the air, pointing directly at him, but her hairpins spoiled the picture. One of them slipped under the weight of her long tresses, and the whole affair came cascading down around her head. 'Don't you dare laugh,' she warned as her hand retreated before the disaster.

'I wouldn't dare,' he agreed. 'So, we tell people that——' He stopped to think for a moment. 'We tell people that we're going to be married from home, Valeria. We—er—plan to use the ballroom. If the sun shines we'll have the service on the lawn. If not, it will be inside. And a reception to follow, at home. I'll have one of my secretaries in Boston run up an impressive guest list.'

'That's just great,' she grumbled. 'And what do I tell all *my* friends?'

'You can't have it two ways,' he chuckled. 'If you want to invite some of your friends to the wedding we're not going to have, you can call this number, and tell Mary who they are that you don't want invited—or do want to—as the case may be.'

'Damn you,' she muttered. The oatmeal was cold, and starting to congeal in the dish.

'Probably,' he sighed. 'Now, is there any other problem? I suppose you could contact some local clergyman to do the deed?'

'You mean—just call him up and lie to him about a wedding that's not going to happen? I can't do that,' she shouted at him. He put a hand over his ear and winced.

'You're just making enquiries,' he suggested tentatively. 'No date has been set, but you want to—you know the routine better than I do.'

'Darned if I do.' She made one more attempt to spoon the oatmeal, and then threw the spoon down in disgust. 'For your information, I've never been married before!' Even under his smooth tan she could see the blood rising. He took the napkin from his lap and set it down beside his unused plate.

'For some reason you're trying to pick a fight this morning, Valeria. Is there something I did last night that upset you?'

She glared at him, the anger showing. Yes, it was something you did last night, you big overgrown bully. You kissed me. Remember that? You went out of your way to turn me on, and then you laughed and walked away. And you knew exactly what you were doing, you—you—and then you left me. Did I sleep last night the way you did? You know darned well I didn't. Who was it that tossed and turned and squirmed all night, and left the pillow-case salt-water wet? Not you, Lothario. Not you. I ought to take that pitcher of orange juice and pour it all over your head. And the only thing that keeps me from doing it is that I haven't the courage!

'So if it wasn't something I did, was it something I said?'

'I'll call the minister,' she said grimly. 'And I'm going off today to get my wedding dress this morning. This afternoon, if the weather clears, I'm going to attend a discussion about the Pilgrim Station nuclear plant.'

'Spend all the money you want.' He waved a hand vaguely in the air. 'Charge it to me. Better still, take one of my credit cards.' He fumbled in his pocket for his wallet, and let the long plastic holder of cards of various types cascade down, in much the way her hair had fallen.

'I'll pay for my own clothes, thank you,' she snapped. 'You don't have to—oh, you are an impossible man! Why anyone would want to *really* marry you I'll never understand!'

'There have been those who have indicated an interest,' he pointed out dolefully as he re-folded his card file. 'More than a couple.' And then he changed the subject. 'You know, I'm glad you're going to this discussion thing. You and I might have to re-think our position on nuclear power. Just the other day the Governor was saying that he's absolutely *against* such plants in settled areas!'

Which was news enough to make Valeria choke on her coffee. She was still coughing when he came around the table, grinned down at her like some lion looking for the best place to bite, and kissed her gently on the forehead. Before she could think of a single nasty thing to say to him, he was gone. His daughter must have met him just outside. She heard the casual salutations, and then Maria wandered in, Rudolph behind her, keeping his nose to the heel of her shoe.

'I've been walking the dog,' the girl said. 'He seems to like splashing along. I think the salt water does his legs some good. But he still tries to chase the crabs out into the mud-flats. Silly.'

'He's long on memory,' Val chuckled. 'There was a time he could easily swim a channel the size of the one in back of the house. Nowadays, I'm afraid if he got stuck on those flats we might lose him. And, Maria, I *do* thank you for paying such attention to my dog.'

'No need to thank me,' the girl replied sombrely. 'Rudolph is about the only one in the house I'm speaking to these days.'

So that's the way the wind blows, Val thought as she watched the girl move to a chair and pour herself a glass of milk. We're in the middle of a truce, but the war still goes on. Maria looked different this morning. Her face was gradually slimming down, and her hair had grown to the point where it was almost even on both sides. Dressed as she was in a neat little shirtwaister, she looked more adult than ever before. The child will grow, Val thought, and in a couple of years she'll have a wonderful figure, be as smart as a whip, and be chasing boys who aren't good enough to shine her shoes.

'I wish we had some of that sausage you served at your house,' Maria said out of the blue.

*'Linguiça?'* Valeria asked, happy to find some neutral subject to talk about. 'That's easy to find. I'm going out today—if I don't drown, I'll get you some.'

'Going out?' Maria's face lighted up. 'Another picket line?'

'Well, not exactly,' Val mused. 'We call it a discussion group. We're going to sit down and discuss the situation at Pilgrim Station.'

'That doesn't sound too interesting,' Maria commented as she helped herself to a double serving of scrambled eggs. 'But then, you don't do that kind of thing,' she said cautiously. 'You're smarter than the average schoolteacher, and the catch in this little discussion is——' She stopped to ruminate, and then her eyes lit up with unholy glee. 'Just where do you plan to do this sitting down and discussing?'

Valeria could not suppress the smile. The girl was altogether too clever. 'Well,' she drawled, 'We thought we would sit down in the middle of Main Street, at the town square. If the rain stops, somewhere round noon, more or less.'

'Holy cow,' Maria laughed. The light, cheerful notes ran up the wall and echoed. 'On Monday during the tourist season? There'll be a monumental traffic mess! I suppose somebody has already alerted the media?'

'Well, of course,' Val returned. 'That's the purpose of the game, to get a little publicity.'

'You know,' the child said slowly, 'I could almost like you, Valeria, if you weren't going to marry my father.'

'I'm—not—going—to—marry—your—father!' Val said very slowly and very carefully. 'Surely he explained all that to you?'

'He came into my room this morning,' Maria admitted. 'And he coughed and hmmphed and mumbled something about "playing a game about weddings", and then he left. I went back to sleep. Because the truth of the matter is that you *are* going to marry him. I know it, and Mrs Baines knows it, and my papa knows it—and—I'm coming with you this morning!'

'Hey, now just wait a minute, young lady. You can't crash the party. Just because nothing happened at that last picket line doesn't mean that you're all of a sudden a great demonstrator. This little operation is going to be highly volatile. It's close enough for all the kooks to gather. Besides, I have to make a stop first to buy something. Something that you *surely* won't like.'

'I'm going with you.' The girl's jaw was set. All the sparkle had gone out of her voice. She's got a mission, Valeria warned herself. For a while there she was Bart Thomas's daughter, but now she's Joan of Arc! And the set of that jaw makes it plain what an uproar there'll be if I turn her down!

'Well, all right,' she sighed. 'Only don't blame me if you don't like it!'

Harry Larper was away with Bart in Boston, so Valeria drove them in her own car, happy to have the freedom of the wheel again. Her goal was Cranberry Crossroads, in Kingston. It was a short drive down almost empty Route Three. It almost seemed as if the slanting rain had driven competitors off the road.

Avril Dene advertised itself as 'the best in women's fashion design'. Valeria sighed as they walked into the showroom. Every tag had a designer-name on it, and she could see the prices going up and up for every step they took. Of course, she had Bart's OK to run up a bill—but not for the life of her would she allow some *man* to dress her. Not a bit. This purchase might murder her savings account, but she would pay for it all herself!

'Madame wishes——?' the saleswoman murmured. Valeria took a deep breath, checked Maria's expectant look out of the corner of her eyes, and took the plunge.

'Madame wishes a wedding dress,' she said firmly. Maria's eyes blazed in anger as the girl slumped into a seat. Well, I *did* try to talk her out of it, Val thought glumly.

'A—formal wedding gown?' The saleswoman, a slight, thin woman of indeterminate age, fluttered around them for a bit. 'Something in white with a train and veil?'

'Good lord, no,' Val responded. Spend all her savings for a dress she could only wear once? If that? That would be the height of stupidity! 'No, I want something nice, but practical. A dress that I can wear *after* the wedding. Something swish and slinky and knee-length—but not too sexy.'

'With a figure like yours,' the woman chuckled, 'I could hang you over with window curtains and still it would turn out sexy.' Maria gave a disgruntled cough. Valeria settled back in a chair next to the child.

'I told you you wouldn't like it,' she muttered out of the side of her mouth.

'You're not married yet,' the girl threatened. Funny, Val thought, we both have the same idea. No, I'm not married yet. Maybe the Lord will send another deluge— or Bart will decide he'd rather be a bank robber than a judge. All about as possible as that the Red Sox would win the World Series!

And so, in the inevitable flow of things, half a dozen dresses were paraded before her, and she hemmed and hawed and finally decided on the simplest of them all.

A plain knee-length dress in ivory—because white clashed with her hair-colour. It was an understated silk thing that was certainly slinky enough. Its high mandarin collar blended into a fluted-lace bodice and a shirred waist, and then swept cleanly out into a floating skirt that swished and swirled more than satisfactorily. In consultation with experts, she added a taffeta petticoat for the rustling sound, and a pair of matching pumps with two-inch heels.

It was an exciting hour, even for so pragmatic a person as Valeria Brewster. And it was not until they brought the bill that she noted the designer label, *Diane Von Furstenburg*, and her almost paralysed fingers wrote the cheque that would keep her on bread and water until Christmas—if not longer.

Back in the car, her boxes stacked in the back seat, Val held off starting the motor for a time. Maria had spoken not a word since that opening statement about marriage had been made.

'Believe me, it's all part of the game,' she told the girl. 'I promised your dad that I'd help him get his judicial appointment. And that's the game we're playing. I'm *not* going to marry him.'

'That's what *you* say,' Maria returned cynically. 'I've been here long enough to recognise what a Pilgrim's promise is worth. Let's go to the demonstration.'

'*I* keep my promises,' Val said doggedly. 'And for your information, I'm not a Pilgrim. Maybe I'd better take you back home and drop you off.'

'Oh, no, you don't.' Maria's voice rose half an octave. Her eyes had that glittery stare in them that almost seemed fanaticism. Valeria had seen that sort of look a time or two in desperate students, just before they blew their cool. 'I came for the fun,' Maria continued, 'and you can't stop me.'

'I can see that you get home,' Valeria snapped.

'And if you do, I'll immediately call the police department,' the girl threatened. No mean threat, that, Val thought. Her little demonstration would require some hundred or more volunteers. If they massed at some point away from the town square, the police would be able to head them off. If they gathered in small groups and moved in, advance notice would allow the law to scatter them. Only by sudden surprise—arriving at the appointed place before the police had notice, could they be truly effective.

'Blackmail isn't a nice thing.' Val acknowledged her defeat bitterly.

'Well, I never said I was a nice person,' Maria said insolently. 'You'd better get going, or we'll be late.'

A spontaneous demonstration required as much planning as a full-scale battle. Valeria, elected by acclamation to be the general of her band of two hundred volunteers, had spent a month of careful work. Groups had been organised by health and age. Starting points had been selected; places where five or ten women might assemble in Plymouth without causing a commotion. The oldest and poorest in health, for example, around the statue of the Pilgrim Maiden, just a few steps from the square. Others, the young and healthy, the brisk walkers, were assigned starting points at the Pilgrim Mother statue, or Plymouth Rock, or the Howland House, or—right under the nose of the police department—at Burial Hill.

Volunteers had long since paced the distance from each assembly point to the square, and recorded the time required to walk the route very sedately.

A van had been volunteered, and was now parked just off the square, manned by two nurse-volunteers and a supply of first-aid equipment. An elderly lawyer had been brow-beaten by his wife, three sisters, and four daughters, and was now standing by outside the police station with a handful of writs tucked in his inside pocket. The judge who had signed the writs, under suitable pressure himself, had found it convenient to go fishing.

Technology had invaded the system, also. Pins and identification cards, portable megaphones and radio receivers, citizens' band radio transmitters, enough so that each group had one. And now, Valeria thought as she tried to park her car on Water Street, all we need is for the rain to stop!

Somebody up there must have been listening. Almost to the second, the clouds to the east parted and a weak and watery August sun blessed the land.

'OK,' Val said. 'Let's go. Turn on the radio to WPLM.' Maria slid out of the car, already designated to carry the radios.

'Why would we want to listen to the radio?' The girl was still encased in anger, but her interest in the operation was piercing tiny holes in her armour.

'Because one of ours is working at the station,' Val chuckled. 'Know thine enemy. That's an old quotation. Use thine enemy's radio station, that's a brand new one. The Japanese thought that one up for Pearl Harbor.' Maria had snapped on the battery-operated transistor radio, and music was floating out. The tape came to an end, and the announcer came on. 'Cherry blossoms, that's what that song reminds me of——' Val flipped the switch off. 'Let's go,' she commanded, and the little group around her started up Brewster Street.

'Cherry blossoms?' Maria had been caught in the group and was only now struggling to catch up.

'Cherry blossoms,' Val said seriously. 'A phrase not likely to be used by accident. It means everything is on schedule, get a move on. You haven't walked through this area before, have you?'

'I—no.' Maria was having trouble with her crisis-management. 'Where are the signs, and stuff like that?'

'In the back of a truck that just had a breakdown in the square,' Val said. 'They have some motor difficulty, and a tow truck won't be able to get to them before noon—and by that time it'll be too late.'

'Phew!' Maria gasped. 'And I thought it was all so easy. You just scribble a few signs and——'

'Experience,' Val commented, waving her hand off to the south. 'That's the Mayflower Society House. You ought to go and tour it some day.'

'I will,' Maria promised. 'Why do they have so many statues?'

'If I say it's for tourism, you'd believe it. And if I told you the truth, you'd doubt it.' Val said. 'The people of Plymouth believe in the town's mystique. This is where it all really started—America's home town. There's a Pilgrim monument, a Massasoit monument, a Pilgrim Mother monument, a Pilgrim Maiden monument, a Plymouth Rock monument—oh, I guess you could go on for hours. Now, remember what I told you. Stick close to me. Do what I do. Don't, for God's sake, look at the spectators or try to talk to them. There will be agitators of all stripes in the crowd, and it only takes a little flame to turn a demonstration into a riot!'

Valeria's eyes were checking the square. Her troops were gathering in fine style. Mostly women, but with a leaven of young men. Those she watched. Women had learned to be placid in the face of taunts; young men had difficulty controlling their anger. Trouble was everywhere, just looking for a place to happen.

Cars were moving up and down Main Street in a steady stream. Sergeant Hoady of the police department was standing negligently at the corner. Val breathed a sigh of relief. She had counted on Sergeant Hoady. He was the old-fashioned kind of cop. Women were creatures that needed to be protected—even from themselves. The good sergeant would never know how much his soft-heartedness was worked into the plan. Val took a deep breath and snatched at Maria's hand. Across the street four of her most dependable assistants were ready, watching her. She took another deep breath and stepped off the kerb.

Automobile brakes squealed. A couple of angry motorists blew their horns. Val and her compatriots marched grandly toward each other with a steady stride, paying no attention to the traffic. In the exact middle of the street they stopped.

'Oh, my!' Sergeant Hoady hurried up to them. 'Not again, Miz Brewster? I thought you promised you wouldn't——'

'I only promised I wouldn't do it on Sunday.' Valeria gave him her best smile, and then swept a hand across her forehead. 'I—don't feel well,' she sighed, in her best Katherine Cornell performance. 'I——' She wavered. Two of her assistants came up to help her as she fell back. They gradually lowered her to the ground. 'Oh, my,' she moaned.

'What is it?' Maria bent over, her childish face perplexed, concerned.

'The street's still wet,' Val whispered to her. 'I forgot about that. We're all going to have wet bottoms.'

'Come on now, Miss Brewster,' the police sergeant pleaded. 'You know you're not ill, and I know you aren't. And you're making a terrible mess of things and—oh, my God.' When he straightened up Sergeant Hoady noticed that fifty or more women had now filled the street, sitting in little groups, talking to each other. And others were coming out of the gathering crowd carrying signs. 'Axe the Atom,' they announced. 'Turn off Plymouth Station.'

'Now, Miz Brewster, you know I can't let you tie up the centre of the city. I'm going to have to call the paddy wagon!'

Valeria patted a place beside her for Maria. The girl looked disgustedly at the puddles, but finally decided to sit. Someone appeared and handed Valeria a megaphone. She passed it to her assistant. Almost immediately a chant arose from the demonstrators. 'Axe the Atom!' It went up the hillside toward the courthouse and police station like an invading army. A flock of pigeons, at home in the tower of old First Church, fluttered away, their wings stirring a thunder.

'Miz Brewster,' the sergeant warned. His face was flushed. The one hand he kept on his club was white with the tension of his grip.

'Your paddy wagon only holds ten people,' Val teased him. 'So you'll need twenty trips. *Axe the Atom!*'

Horns were blaring in very direction. Sergeant Hoady had no need to call anyone. Even the desk-sergeant up the hill in the police station could tell what was going on. Reinforcements were pouring out of the building. But Plymouth, with something over twenty thousand residents, did not have the biggest police force in the world, and the attention of eight more officers was spread very thin. ''Axe the Atom!'' The cry went up from all sides as signs were waved and demonstrators took turns chanting.

'It's going to be a very satisfactory lunch time,' Valeria commented, proud of their achievement. She flipped on the radio tuned to the local station. 'Traffic is backed up as far as Cherry Street in the north end,' the announcer was saying. 'The county sheriff's office is sending in patrols. The office of the local council has announced that the town will not allow this blatant attempt to influence their actions. All participants will be punished to the full extent of the law!' She flipped the switch off and grinned at Maria.

The girl was huddled beside her, head down, a petulant look on her face. For a moment the success turned sour in Valeria's mouth. The girl was up to something— but before Val had a chance to probe, to see what lay behind all this, two newspaper reporters and a television team pushed their way through the crowd and demanded answers from her. The camera-eye panned the street as pairs of policemen tried to lift the supine women and carry them off. It was difficult. Even a small woman, all her muscles relaxed, not co-operating at all, was a hard bundle to move.

But there were other, more impatient faces in the crowd. 'I don't believe it,' Val muttered. 'Skinheads!' Here and there in the crowd young men were gathering, heading directly for the centre of the demonstration. One of the newest phenomena in American street life, they were young toughs, neo-Nazis, who shaved their heads to distinguish them from the common population. And here they were, moving purposefully through the crowd, swinging handfuls of chains, and headed directly towards her. It was time to be the leader again.

'Remember what I told you,' she cautioned Maria, and then stood up. Sergeant Hoady had long since been swept away. Four of the men surrounded her. Men indeed, she thought as she looked them over. Eighteen years old, no more. And she knew three of them. They were drop-outs from the high school. Bitter young men who, even in this era of high employment, could not find a job that satisfied them. And now they formed a square around her.

The voices on the square went silent as all eyes fastened on the confrontation.

'Well, if it ain't Miss Do-Good,' one of the boys taunted. Following her own orders, she looked at them, and said nothing.

'Somebody ought to take you out in the bush and——' Whatever he was about to suggest was not going to be too pleasant, but Valeria never heard it. While she was concentrating on maintaining her cool, someone behind her planted both hands in the middle of her back and gave her a massive push. She bounced off the shoulder of one of the men. He pulled back his chains in a frightened reaction. A roar went up all over the square. Something struck Valeria Brewster on the side of her face, and everything went black. The riot lasted for over an hour.

Bart Thomas shoved his hands in his carefully tailored pockets, and leaned one hip on the corner of the desk. The governor's office was tucked in a corner of the old General Court building, high up under the golden dome. People were in and out in a mad confusion, but the white-haired lady at the desk was an effective traffic director, and through the open door into the inner office he could see that things were proceeding smoothly.

Malcolm Graves came bustling out. 'The chief justice will be another five minutes, Judge.' Graves grinned up at him. A small, slim man, much in the governor's image.

'Then they voted?' he asked. It was hard to control the excitement building up in him. It had been a long wait. Not just this morning, feeling like an odd bookend in the office, but the whole four weeks that had been required to bring everything to a head.

'They voted,' Graves assured him. 'A unanimous vote. We seem to have been very effective against Senator Poitras.'

'*You* must have,' Bart told him. 'I never could talk to that idiot!'

'Now, now,' Graves chuckled. 'One mustn't speak ill of the dead. The senator has been dead from the neck up for the past twenty years. Ah, here comes the chief justice now. We only have six minutes scheduled for the swearing-in.'

The bulky, white-haired man who stalked in was well known through the state. As the chief judiciary of the Commonwealth, he had served long and well. The trio swept into the inner office. The governor put down his gold pen and looked up at them.

'Well, we did it.' He nodded a welcome at them all. 'It's time we're able to get some eminently qualified men on the Bench, Judge Thomas——' He might have planned to say something else, but his telephone rang at just that moment. The governor looked surprised. Un-announced telephone calls were *never* put through in *his* administration. But he had been raised in the telephone age. When the bell rings, you pick it up. It was almost like a saliva-response.

'What?' he said into the telephone. 'No, I'm not your father, young lady, and I—oh!'

'For you, Judge,' he laughed as he handed the telephone along to Bart. 'Your daughter? I guess she's entitled to be the first to congratulate you.'

Bart put the phone to his ear as he offered the assembled group an apologetic smile. 'Papa? It's me!'

'Of course it is,' he chuckled, and then realised that the girl was almost in tears. 'What's the matter, love?'

'I—uh—Papa, I'm in jail!'

'*What?* They can't put you in jail, you're a legal minor. Did you tell them you were only thirteen?'

'They wouldn't believe me, Papa. They said if I was old enough to—to do that—I was old enough to be in jail!'

'Well, dear God,' he roared. 'I'm all tied up here just at the moment. Call Valeria. She'll straighten it out!'

'I can't do that.' Maria had reverted to adolescence in a hurry. He could hear the tears. 'They said I could only make one telephone call.'

'Don't worry,' he soothed. 'I'm sure our Miss Brewster will come and straighten everything out. Our little Pilgrim is a great one for that. What in the world did you do to get arrested? Parking in front of a hydrant?'

The girl was fighting her tears, with some success. 'No hydrant,' she reported. 'This—man—he went after Valeria—and so I hit him on the head with my radio transmitter. They say he's still in the hospital.'

'Oh, lord.' He added a few rounded Slavic words. Short ones. 'And just where the hell is the woman I pay to look after you?'

'She's—she's in the hospital, too.' The words slid down the long telephone line like a repentant sigh.

'I'm coming,' her father said desperately. 'I'm coming. Right this damn minute!' He felt as if his stomach had just been ripped open. His daughter in jail was not an insurmountable problem. But Valeria in the hospital, that was a different matter indeed. He returned the handset.

'My daughter's in jail,' he told the throng. 'And my fiancée is in the hospital. I can't wait for the ceremony. I've got to go!'

He was already moving before the assembled group could say anything. The governor looked at his chief secretary and grinned. Two newsmen who had been invited for the ceremony dived for the pay telephones in the hall.

The chief justice, who had lived through more storm and strife than most, followed Bart out into the outer office, and trailed behind him as he went out into the corridor. 'It's a slow elevator,' he said prosaically. 'Raise your right hand. Repeat after me. I, Bartholomew Thomas, do solemnly swear——'

# CHAPTER NINE

VALERIA came home from Jordan hospital the next day. 'She has a big bump on her head,' Doctor Emfield told Bart when he came to pick her up. 'We were afraid of concussion, but she apparently is going to be OK. I would say, let her take it easy for a day or two, but if she has headaches, call me immediately.'

'I will,' Bart promised solemnly. 'And believe me, from here on in I'll watch her like a hawk.'

'Takes after her grandma,' the doctor chuckled. 'I was her family physician for many a year. Strong-willed woman, Grandma Brewster was. I hear you plan to marry the girl?'

'Do you hear that?' Bart smiled back, but as he hurried down to the lobby to await delivery of the patient there was a little worry furrow on his forehead, because he had no idea exactly how he was going to go about it.

There weren't many words spoken on the trip. 'Damn fool idea,' he muttered as he made the jagged turn into Coles Lane.

'So occasionally I make a mistake,' she returned weakly. 'My head is in no condition to have you ringing a peal over it. What I need is a good lawyer. How's Maria?'

'You've got a good lawyer. I don't intend to ring any peals over you. I did think vaguely about ringing your neck, but I gave that up. Maria is—well, you'll see. She wants to talk to you as soon as you get home.'

Sandwich Street was crowded with traffic. It took him several minutes before he could make the left turn. He used part of the time to think, the other part to observe. 'That left eye of yours is going to be a beauty,' he commented finally as a break opened in the traffic flow.

'It'll impress the kids in my first class next week,' she said determinedly. 'I'll be a hero. Are they going to put me in jail?'

'I doubt it,' he grumbled as they came up on Cobbs Hollow Lane, and he turned up into the driveway of the house. 'I promised to sue the city—in your name, of course—for one million dollars.'

'On what grounds?' she gasped, and turned to stare at him. The sudden movement hurt her head. She grabbed at it with both hands. He brought the car to a gentle stop.

'Grounds? We'll think about that later. Right now the town fathers are trying to find a hole to hide in. What an idiot operation—Axe the Atom indeed!'

He sat in the seat, drumming his fingers on the steering wheel. 'You know, you've practically blown my whole plan to get a seat on the Bench, don't you?'

'I—I'm sorry.' Remorse dripped on every syllable. He checked out of the corner of his eyes. She was hunched over, staring straight out of the windscreen, with a tremendous elastic bandage holding an ice-bag on the top of her head. He had never seen her look so miserable. Now was the time to press the issue.

'So there's no escape now,' he grumbled. 'We are going to go ahead with the wedding. The doctor said you should rest for a couple of days. On Thursday we get married.'

'No way,' she muttered but her heart wasn't in it. Such a scandal. And all her fault. Still, a girl who let herself get railroaded into marriage was some kind of a fool. She drew up what little courage she had. 'No way!' she said firmly. 'Listen carefully. I'm speaking English. I am not going to marry you!'

'Out of the car and up to bed,' he ordered peremptorily as he climbed out on his side and slammed the driver's door. When he came around to hold her door for her she slid out cautiously, more afraid of him than of banging her head. When he moved behind her to close the door she sidled away, crabwise, and kept an eye on him.

'I told you I decided not to strangle you,' he repeated sternly. 'Mabel's waiting. Get yourself to bed.'

'Am I supposed to kiss your foot?' she asked with a strained voice.

'It would be appropriate,' he gruffed at her. 'But your head is liable to fall off if you do. Up to bed!'

And, like the good little spineless, half-terrified girl you are, she told herself, let's up-to-bed. An hour later, having been helped into the big, soft bed, fed a cup of weak tea, two more pills, and had her ice-bag changed, she settled back against the pillows and assessed the situation.

So here I am. One over-aged virgin, surrounded by luxury and pretending to hate every bit of it. Because that's what you're doing, Valeria. He's a—very acceptable man—in some things. Good-looking, young enough, employed—a smile worked its way through to her tired face. That had always been Gran's summation. Girls have to be beautiful—boys only need be employed! Dear Gran. She would have loved this man! He's so darned arrogant!

His daughter? Maria had so many quirks, she was harder to follow than a corkscrew. One thing's for sure, she hates me. A thirteen-year-old witch? If she can cast spells, I'm dead.

His ambition. It sounded reasonable enough. He's made his packet in this world, and now he wants to fulfil a pledge to his father. How about *that*! 'Convict's Son Sits On High Bench'! What a headline *that* would be. But I've definitely put paid to that ambition—unless marriage could paper over the crack in his political foundation?

A platonic marriage, followed quickly by an annulment? One banana split, two spoons please? I read too many Regency romances. What is it that bothers you, schoolteacher? The platonic part—or the quick annulment part—or both? Warily her mind skirted around *that* thought and let it lay there.

Summary. You've done him a very bad turn, Valeria Brewster. You owe it to them both—he and Maria—to do whatever you can to make it up. So, if you go ahead with these wedding plans, who knows—in the two days involved, the governor's council might just meet and cast their vote for him and—and once he's taken the oath, he can never be fired. Well, almost never. He would have life tenure!

And if the council doesn't vote in the next two days? 'I don't want to think about that,' she muttered, and resolutely went off to sleep.

Valeria awoke with the late afternoon sun shining in her eyes, feeling much better. A shadow cast across the bed turned out to be Maria, sitting disconsolately in the big, upholstered chair. Valeria ordered her hand to move, and to her surprise, it did. The girl gasped.

'Oh! You're awake!'

Val turned her head slowly, pleased to see that it was not going to fall off. 'Yes, I believe I am,' she said. Her throat was dry, and it was hard to form the words. 'You've been crying again, Maria?'

'Oh—Valeria!' The child seemed overcome by something. Fear, tension, guilt? It was hard to tell.

Valeria lifted one hand and beckoned. The girl slipped out of the chair to her knees and laid her head on Val's chest. She was shaking uncontrollably. Val's hand moved gently across her back and patted. 'It can't be that bad, child. Tell me about it.'

'Valeria,' the girl sobbed, 'I've been a fool. I didn't mean for you to be hurt—truly I didn't!'

'I know you didn't, love. Tell me about it. Everything.'

The dry, hacking sobs gradually came to a halt. Maria lifted her head and moved back on her haunches by the bed, her eyes glued to the huge bandage on Valeria's head.

'It's only there to hold the ice-bag,' Valeria commented as she slowly unwound the bandage and took off the cold pack. 'See?'

'But—they've cut off a whole circle of your hair—and there's a bump—oh, what have I done?'

It was all a surprise to Valeria. She felt gingerly for the bump. Sure enough, some of her mass of hair had been amputated to allow the doctor access to the skin. 'Well, I've got more than enough hair to cover it,' she said, trying to soothe the child.

'I wouldn't feel so bad if you hadn't got hurt,' Maria stammered. 'And, to tell the truth, if it had worked. But it didn't. Isn't that something? If you do a bad thing, and it works, you don't mind so much having to *do* badness—do you?'

Which was enough twisted logic to make even a schoolteacher wince. Valeria did. 'Why don't you explain it all to me, one word at a time?' she sighed. 'I seem to be particularly dense this afternoon.'

'Well, it was really *your* idea,' Maria pointed out morosely. 'It seemed to me that if Papa didn't get to be a judge, everything would work out all right. He wouldn't *have* to get married, and sooner or later he and my mom would get together again, and everything would be OK, because I was sure this thing about my mother marrying must be strictly Hollywood hype. So, I tried to figure out what would stop him from being a judge. Remember, you said how easy it was to start a riot when a crowd is assembled? I figured that if I could start a riot—a very small riot——' Valeria grinned. Like starting a forest fire, creating a *very small* riot was a sometime thing!

The girl took a deep breath and plunged head-first into the rest of the explanation. 'There were plenty of media people there, and I thought if I were arrested in the middle of a riot that it would get in all the papers and then Papa wouldn't get the appointment and everything would be fine again, so when they arrested me I told them my name and said I was twenty-one, and they believed me and they locked me up——' a pause for breath was required '—but then I found out that it wasn't a *little* riot at all and that you were in the hospital and I just didn't know what to do and the police wouldn't tell me how you were and I thought you were killed and I called Papa and *he* wasn't too happy and——' And the flood-gates broke as the tears washed the words away. Maria's head collapsed on Valeria's breast again, and for ten minutes the pair consoled each other.

'There, now,' Val coaxed when the storm was over. 'You just sit down here and relax, and we'll see if we can promote some chicken soup. I understand it has great restorative qualities.'

'You're not mad at me?' Maria just could not believe it. 'If I was you and you was me, I'd still be mad! Plenty mad!'

'Well, I'm not,' Val promised. 'Not a bit. I'm just stiff and sore and—I think I've got a dandy of a black eye!'

'I've seen worse,' Maria reported after a thorough check-up. 'Not many worse, but some.' She took Valeria's hand and cherished it. 'Do you suppose—after all this trouble I've been—that we could be—well, friends?'

'I suppose we could,' Val replied solemnly. 'And I'm *not* going to marry your father.'

On Wednesday afternoon she felt well enough to be out of bed, but not out of the bedroom. Mrs Baines appeared just after lunch with the box containing Val's wedding dress. 'We have to try it on for size,' the housekeeper insisted.

'Why do we *have* to?' Val queried.

'Because *he* said so.' There was no need to query about which 'he' it was that said so. They both understood. So Valeria fumbled her way into the dress and managed a passable demonstration, without any argument.

'Not bad,' Mabel said, her head cocked to one side as she examined every stitch and seam.

'It better *not* be,' Val threatened. 'You should see the price I paid for this. I'm going to have to wear it twice a week for the next school term. And I'm not sure how it'll go over with the school principal. That mandarin collar makes me look something like Fu Manchu!'

'Don't be silly,' Mrs Baines clucked. 'You only have to wear it once. And there's only *one* man you have to please.'

'I keep telling everybody around here,' Val said, exasperated, 'I'm *not* going to marry that man!'

'Yes, of course,' Mrs Baines replied absent-mindedly. 'Maybe we could take a little tuck up here?'

'No, we can *not*.' Valeria brushed Mabel's hands away from her bodice. 'I don't intend to parade around with half of me hanging out! I'm not Amelé Poitras.'

'And thank God for that,' the housekeeper agreed. 'Reverend Saltmarsh from the Congregational Church has agreed to come and do the service. Ten o'clock tomorrow morning. You should see the ballroom. I had a contractor in. It's all shiny and beautiful.'

'Better have a snack available for the reverend,' Valeria groused. 'He's going to be pretty angry, coming all this way for nothing!'

After dinner that night, everyone seemed to tiptoe around Valeria. Every argument—and she tried to pick at least two with every inmate of the house—was turned aside with smiles and kind words. Bart especially was playing 'out-of-sight'. She caught occasional glimpses of him turning corners, but when she hustled to catch up he was always gone.

And so to bed. But not to sleep. Valeria was tired, but every time she dropped off she fell into the same little dream. She was walking slowly up the aisle on Harry's arm, in her nightgown and bare feet. They stopped in front of the altar, where an over-sized Bart Thomas waited for her, licking his lips. The preacher said 'Do

you, Valeria Whatchamacallit take this man to be——'
And at that point she screamed 'No!' And promptly
woke up.

Over and over this little tape played, until she gave it
all up, and for the sake of her mental health got up out
of bed and went to sit on the window-seat. The moon
was in its third quarter, but bright enough to light the
bay. The waves were small, with not a white-cap to be
seen. The moon and the waves—they spread a sort of
peace into which she could relax. Through all the confusion, piercing it like a sharp knife, she heard a voice.
A well-remembered, well-loved voice. Gran.

'He's really a nice man,' the voice said. 'None of them
are perfect. Yes, he's arrogant—like your grandfather.
And just a little bit stuffy. But nothing a good wife
couldn't straighten out. He has a lot of good points. He
loves his daughter, and his work—and who knows who
else. He's kind to Rudolph, and to everybody else in the
house. He's steadily employed——'

And that brought a giggle. Gran's favourite bromide.
But it didn't matter, for she suddenly realised it wasn't
Gran who was speaking, but herself. If *everything* goes
wrong, she told herself, it still won't be *all* bad. If the
council doesn't vote before ten o'clock, well—it will be
only platonic. Isn't that what he said originally?

Valeria Brewster hugged herself and went back to bed,
wondering if this might be the last night in all her life
that her name would be Brewster.

Mrs Baines woke her up at eight o'clock with a cheery
'Good morning, all!' as she opened the curtains and let
the day stream in. 'Sunshine, my dear.'

'Good morning, all?' Val repeated grumpily. Waking up early was not her favourite indoor sport. 'Are we a crowd?'

'Don't be a spoilsport,' Mabel chuckled. 'I brought you breakfast. A bride needs something in her stomach on the day!'

Valeria sat up indignantly. 'I've *got* something in my stomach already,' she snapped. 'I don't know whether its ulcers or indigestion pains. I am *not* getting married today!'

'Of course not,' Mrs Baines agreed as she smoothed the sheets and placed the tray over Val's knees. 'Now eat up——'

'I'm too old for "there's a good girl",' Val complained. 'And I can't eat all this. I'm not a horse!'

'Having a little trouble, are we?' Bart Thomas came in without knocking and walked over beside the bed.

'Oh, bad luck,' Mrs Baines wailed. 'You're not supposed to see the bride today until she comes to you.'

'If I wait that long,' he said, 'she'll die of hunger. Aren't you eating your breakfast, Valeria?'

'No, she is not,' Mabel exclaimed. 'She's giving me a hard time!'

'Is she really?' He came closer and bent over the bed to kiss her forehead. 'This is the day,' he said in a strong and commanding voice. 'And pretty soon is the hour. Eat your breakfast, Valeria Brewster!'

'You can't make me,' she whispered indecisively. 'And you can't make me marry you!'

'Oh, can't I?' He dropped to one knee by the bed, putting his eyes at the same level as hers. Big, dark eyes, sparkling as if the Devil were encased in them, with his trident at the ready. Determined eyes. If you fall into them you'll drown for sure, she told herself as she struggled to escape his spell.

'Valeria?' The deep baritone challenge reinforced the spell. She picked up her fork and ate everything on the tray.

From that point on, the day seemed to fade out of focus for her. Her world was like an arty movie, where nothing was clear, and everything moved through clouds of mist, with orchestra music behind it.

Out of this haze Maria appeared, neatly and conservatively dressed in white. Mrs Baines returned to help her into her wedding dress. The taffeta slip rustled, and at the sight of it the family of finches on the windowsill sent up a barrage of cheers. The mandarin collar turned out to be an inch too tight, restricting her field of vision to straight ahead. A good thing, she told herself. The less I see, the less can frighten me. Why is it that I'm all of a sudden a bunch of nerves? I've been Miss Practical for all my life, and now suddenly in the last few days I've lost control of the ship! I'm *not* going to marry that man!

Every time the telephone rang she knew it had to be the governor with her reprieve—a statement that the council had voted on his nomination. *That* telephone call never came—but Harry did, resplendent in morning-coat and white tie.

'It's time to go down,' he announced. His hoarse voice sounded like an executioner, announcing a date with the electric chair. She put her pale, cold hand on his arm and floated down the stairs, shaking so hard that her teeth chattered.

Mrs Baines was waiting at the foot of the stairs. Deep in her daze, Valeria heard voices without bodies. 'She's never going to make it this way.' And then another. 'Here, drink this.'

She opened her mouth obediently and fire trickled down her throat and burned a hole in her stomach. But it also provided courage. 'Let's go, he's waiting,' another strange voice said.

And *that* will never do, she thought wildly. Making *him* wait? Dear God, no! And so she tried to hurry, but managed only to trip over her own feet. Maria and Harry rescued her.

They came into the ballroom on the far side, near the french doors, which were all open to let in the beauty of the day. The room was flowers, from wall to wall. In fact, the walls had disappeared under the decorations. Smells tantalised her nostrils. She could not *see* clearly, but she could sniff with no trouble. A big, wide room, the walls lined with people, the centre completely empty, and at the far end an altar decked with flowers, and *he* was waiting.

Music played, taped selections feeding through the household amplifier system. She could hear the noise, but not the sound. Her mind seemed to be locked on a montonic channel—everything looked and sounded grey.

The party skated across the glassy surface of the ballroom, Maria leading the way. And suddenly they had arrived. Harry transferred her hand to Bart's. She could vaguely see him frown at the coldness of her palm. He drew her closer, half supporting her. Her mind went blank for a time, and then there was a pause. Reverend Saltmarsh was looking at her over the tops of his half-spectacles. 'Do you, Valeria Anna Brewster, take Bartholomew to be your——'

And at that point her vision cleared. Everything fell into sharp focus. A little door in her mind opened, and sent a cascade of bright beams throughout all the musty corners of her brain, and everything became clear. *I love him,* she yelled at herself. *I love him!*

The good reverend had come to the closure. '—till death do you part?' A Pilgrim's promise, she thought fiercely. Till death do us part. Or longer. Into the moment of silence she mustered all her strength to calm her nerves, looked up at the big, serious-visaged man whose attention was all on her, and in a firm voice she said, 'I do!'

They held the reception in the same ballroom. Chairs marched themselves in under the hand of a million caterers. Tables appeared and were instantly covered with food. A bar opened in each of the four corners of the great room. The first person to come up to congratulate them was the Governor.

'I always thought you were taller,' she said as he kissed her cheek.

'Television has a way of doing that,' the governor returned. 'You are a beautiful lady. I congratulate you, Bartholomew, and wish you both happiness!'

'I waited all morning for you to call,' Valeria blurted out.

'Did you? There was no need. I was coming anyway,' the Governor said in a kindly tone, and then moved along.

'I don't understand either side of that conversation,' her husband said, leaning over to catch her ear above the din of a roomful of conversation.

'No,' she sighed. 'It was very complicated. I'll explain it all some day.' She might have added something else, but she heard him mutter 'Holy crow,' under his breath.

A strange couple were approaching across the polished floor.

The man was rather rotund, stuffed into a shiny black double-breasted suit, his face a brilliant red—from the exertion, perhaps, Val thought. The woman was tall and thin. Five foot eight, brilliantly blonde, waving expressive hands to match her chatter as she came.

'Eleanore,' Bart warned her. 'My former wife.'

Valeria looked around, but Maria had disappeared, last seen diving for the luncheon meats. She shrugged her shoulders and turned back to follow the next act in the play.

'Bart,' Eleanore trilled. Her voice was just a shade too shrill. Given enough power, it might well break all the glasses in the room. Except that they're plastic cups, not glasses, Valeria's pragmatic mind announced.

'Bart, my dear. We were in Boston and thought we would pop in. Let me introduce George Stanhope, my—er—husband. George is a famous Hollywood producer.'

'I'm sure he is,' Bart said, extending a massive hand. Stanhope hesitated before entrusting his paw to the monster in front of him. One never knew what first husbands would do. 'A pleasure,' he grunted.

'And you must be——' The blonde turned toward Valeria and smiled blankly.

'Valeria Thomas,' Val replied, and very carefully put her hands behind her back.

'Valeria—of course,' Eleanore said, and then immediately dismissed her as of no importance. 'Bart,' she continued in her cheery little shriek. 'I hear tell that you've done very well lately!'

'Of course I have,' he returned. He was doing his best to maintain a solemn face, but Val could see the muscles twitching at the corner of his mouth, which brought a smile to her own. 'I managed to catch Valeria, didn't I?'

'Oh——' Eleanore waved the comment off. 'I didn't mean that. I mean where it *counts*! Money. The rumour mills have it that you're very well fixed these days!'

'I'm afraid that's true.' He looked down at Valeria for a moment, and tucked her hand under his arm again before he turned back to Eleanore. 'You divorced me three years too soon. The stock market took a rocket rise, and I rode it all the way to the top.'

Eleanore bit her lip. One of the actors was not playing by the script. But she had come to make a pitch, and make it she would. 'George has just come on a most astounding movie script,' she announced gleefully. 'A real-life tale. Just right for my first starring role. And I think there's just room for you to have a piece of the action. Shall we say——' She looked over at her new husband questioningly.

'Say in the neighbourhood of two hundred and fifty thousand dollars,' the producer said gruffly.

'Nice neighbourhood,' Bart commented. 'What the hell?'

There was a stir in the conversation at the far end of the room. Valeria squinted to see at who and what. Maria was hurrying across the room anxiously, her arms full of Rudolph, who for once was not struggling at all. But he *was* covered from head to toe with mud. Only the grey of his muzzle was *not* covered. And naturally, when a girl in a bright new dress picks up a heavy old dog such as Rudolph, she becomes very muddy too. Not only the dress, of course. She was mud up almost to her knees.

'What happened?' Valeria asked gently. The girl came to a stop in front of the four of them, eyes only on the bride.

'He finally did it,' she almost shouted. 'He wandered off into the mud-flats. If I hadn't seen him he would have been—drowned in the mud. Uggh!'

Not until that moment did Maria notice Eleanore. There was a flash of recognition and shock in her eyes as she turned slowly toward her natural mother. Very gently the girl put Rudolph down on the floor. The old dog's claws scrabbled on the polished surface for a moment, and then Harry was there, sweeping the animal up and disappearing with him.

Maria looked at Eleanore. Valeria, watching, could read tension in every line of the child's body. She was leaning just slightly forward in Eleanore's direction, her hands half raised, an appeal on her face that bespoke past love and single-minded affection.

Eleanore Stanhope looked at her daughter for a moment, as if they both were strangers. Her new husband took one quick look at the girl and blanched. Maria took one tiny step toward her natural mother, and Eleanore screamed, 'Oh, no! Not with all that mud!' and backed away.

In the game of life, you often receive only one chance to throw the dice. Eleanore had just thrown hers. Maria's hands dropped slowly to her sides, and the frantic appeal on her face faded. Very slowly, like a soldier on parade, she turned to face Valeria again. A tiny smile formed on the girl's face, as she just looked.

Without thinking, Valeria raised both her hands in welcome. With a shout, Maria threw herself into the hug, nestled as close as she could get, mud and all, and began to cry. 'I was scared, but I knew I had to get him 'cause he's your dog——' And then there was a long moment of silence, and one more word was added through the tears. 'Mama,' she cried softly, and offered a squeeze to match!

# CHAPTER TEN

IT WAS her wedding night. The party was over, the guests gone, the ballroom cleared and cleaned, and it was time for all good brides to go to bed. Bart escorted her upstairs, tall and quiet and solemn, one arm under her elbow. To the door of her old room they went; he threw it open for her, and offered a slight bow. 'Platonic,' he said.

Val stumbled across the threshold, seething with anger as the door thudded closed behind her. Not a thing had changed. Everything had been exactly as he had said, and now came the *coup de grâce*: 'Platonic.' Complete in her new-found knowledge of herself, Valeria Thomas threw herself down on the bed without undressing, and managed to cry herself to sleep.

Friday morning dawned dull and blustery. Summer was fast fading away. By Labor Day, the great national holiday that fell on the first Monday of September, the hot season would be put behind them and the cool winds would begin to usher in the wildly beautiful colours of autumn. New England dressed in its best in autumn, as the foliage ran the gamut from oak-red to maple-yellow, and all the shades between. Valeria went down to breakfast, to find the dining-room empty. She shrugged her shoulders and made her way to the kitchen.

Mabel Baines was hard at work on a recalcitrant leg of lamb. 'Can't do a thing with it,' the housekeeper commented. 'Needs a mite of marinating. You don't look so good, Mrs T.'

'I've had a hard night,' she returned glumly, and then looked startled as the housekeeper broke out into the loudest guffaws Val had ever heard. The laughter rang until tears came to Mabel's eyes. When she wiped them away the housekeeper became all practicality.

'You need a lot of sustenance,' she insisted. 'Sit down here and I'll whip you up some pancakes. Real maple syrup, too. He gets it right from Vermont, you know.

'Right from the horse's mouth—I mean, tree's mouth? Why do I need a lot of—what you said?'

'Because being a bride requires a lot of stamina,' Mabel asserted. There was a wicked little gleam in her eyes as she turned to the stove. Valeria shrugged her shoulders and sat where commanded. There were too many things going clear over her head these days, but she loved pancakes, so she put the mystery away for future examination.

Maria bounced in about ten minutes later. The girl had her priorities right. 'Oh, pancakes,' she giggled. 'I love pancakes. Good morning, Mabel. Good morning, Mama.' She pulled out the chair next to Valeria's and sank into it. 'I had such wonderful dreams last night. Are you really my mama now?'

'It depends.' Val approached the idea cautiously. This was the new Maria Thomas. 'If you want me to be, then yes, I'm your mama.'

'Stepmother,' Mrs Baines corrected with a grin as she delivered another stack of cakes.

'Wicked stepmother,' Bart contributed as he walked in and sat down. Ideas seemed to run in the Thomas family; he had the same priorities. 'Pancakes? Great. I love pancakes. Good morning, Maria—Mabel.'

And nothing for me, Valeria asked herself? After all I've done for——

'And good morning to you, wife,' he said softly as he leaned over and kissed her full on the lips. It wasn't the most sensual of kisses—but then, at the breakfast table— what more could a girl expect? It *was* warm and moist and comfortable, and—and what he got from her in return was flavoured with maple syrup!

'I don't take much to being called the wicked stepmother,' she said firmly. 'There's a lot that goes on in this family that has to change!'

'New broom,' Maria chuckled. She looked at her father. He returned the gaze. Both of them had a wickedly teasing little gleam in their eyes.

'Cinderella,' her father commented as he took a mouthful of pancake and then tried to shift it out of the way of the conversation. 'What happened to that glamorous lady of yesterday?'

'She stayed too late at the ball,' Valeria stated emphatically. 'Women can't be glamorous morning, noon and night, you know. What you see is what you get!'

'What a good idea,' he muttered. Valeria blushed madly. Naturally he would have to assign the worst possible meaning to every word, she thought. So I'm not glamorous. Who looks glamorous coming down to breakfast in nightgown and old green robe? So maybe I should have done up my hair instead of just leaving it in braids. And maybe I should have used a little lipgloss. Or maybe I should go and jump off the edge of a cliff! Change the subject before they run over you, she commanded herself frantically.

'I'll be going back to my own house today,' she announced. Silence settled in the kitchen. Mabel stood there with the skillet half raised, Maria's mouth dropped open, and Bart's eyes took on that hooded look.

'And may I ask why?' he said gently.

Valeria licked her lips nervously. There was something about his attitude that—frightened her. But only for a moment. She gathered up all the shreds of Brewster courage and looked him straight in the eye.

'Because next week school starts. I have to get my lesson plans together. They're all at the other house. And besides, the house probably needs cleaning. That's what I thought I would do today.'

'Can I help, Mama?' Maria looked every inch a thirteen-year-old at that moment. Watchdog, Valeria told herself. She's accepted me, and now she doesn't mean for me to escape. Another disturbance in her life would be one too many. Am I trapped again?

'There's no need of either of you going over there,' Bart interjected. Again that soft, caressing tone, that hypnotic compulsion. 'I've already told the school committee.'

Panic broke through the compulsion. 'You—told the school committee?'

'I told the school committee that my wife would require some time off. Perhaps a year's sabbatical. They agreed.'

'You—told—them—*what*?'

'A year's sabbatical,' he repeated. 'Watch my lips, wife. A year off!'

'You can't do that,' Valeria complained weakly.

'A husband had a great many rights and powers,' he responded gravely. 'If you want, I'll draw up a legal paper for you on that subject.'

'No,' she said meekly. 'No, thank you. But a whole year? How can I—I don't have that much money left. I couldn't live a full year without——'

'Among other things, husbands are supposed to support their wives.' That wicked grin again. She could hardly decide whether to kiss him or kill him. 'In the manner to which she would like to become accustomed,' he finished.

'You're—I—I've got to go and get dressed,' she sighed as she scraped back her chair and retreated to the privacy of her own room.

'Dinner'll be late tonight, love,' Mabel announced as Val came in from her long walk up the beach with Rudolph. Too long, in fact. The old dog was dragging his tail. Doing his best to look as if he were enjoying himself, but plainly down to his last step or two. 'You two look a sight for sore eyes.'

Val managed a smile and turned to the mirror in the hall. Her long wine-red hair had been blown free by the wind, and surrounded her heart-shaped face like a silken web. Her blouse fitted just a smidgin too tightly. Her jeans were weathered to a uniform grey. And the walk had added colour to her cheeks; colour that matched her hair almost, and contrasted with her sparkling green eyes.

'What's the great man up to now?' she asked jauntily. 'Gone to Boston, I suppose?' Strange, just by commenting on his absence called her attention to it—and upset her heart just a little bit. He was—nice to have around. And if I have to put up with this—platonic— marriage for a year, she thought, I might as well find *something* nice about him. I can't spend all that time being stepmother to his lovely daughter.

'Oh, he said something about some ceremony in Boston,' Mabel said absent-mindedly as she concentrated on the flower arrangement in the hall.

Another blow below the belt! Val grimaced and turned away from the too-revealing mirror. 'So the governor's council finally confirmed him?' It was hard to keep the excitement out of her voice. Excitement and—fear. Was Valeria Thomas about to become the shortest-running play of Broadway? The idea even tasted bad.

'I don't know about those things,' Mabel replied placidly. 'I learned a long time ago not to struggle with the details of Bart's life. He's a volatile man. Are you settling in?'

In what? Val wanted to say. In the mess I've made of my life? Good heavens, I'm already over my head! Think of something else. That's all I seem to do these days is run around trying to change the subject!

'Do you save old newspapers?' she asked abruptly. The housekeeper looked at her as if she had lost all her marbles.

'Old newspapers?'

'Yes. I'm one of these intellectuals, you know. A sucker for the comic strip, *Hagar the Horrible*. And I've missed four nights of it. Monday, Tuesday, Wednesday, and Thursday. I thought maybe if you hadn't thrown them out, I could——'

'I'll look in the kitchen,' Mabel promised. 'If I find them, I'll leave them on your bed.'

The idea was swallowed up in the excitement as Maria came back from her afternoon at the yacht club with the boy next door, a fifteen-year-old by the name of George Plantan. Almost immediately afterward her father and Harry arrived back from Boston.

They were a real family, gathered at the table that night. The leg of lamb had not come up to specifications. The table was laden with thick juicy T-bone steaks, heaps of mashed potatoes, and bowls of tossed salad. Maria had a million things to say about boats. Unfortunately for him, George Plantan rated only one brief sentence. His little yawl was more appreciated than he was. But then again, Val thought, his yawl doesn't have acne and a voice that can't decide whether it's tenor or bass!

When Maria ran out of steam, her father added a few notes. 'I'm going to be on circuit,' he announced, 'for the first six months. So I'll be away from the house for a time. You two will have to look after each other.'

'Then you *did* get confirmed,' Val asked anxiously. Her brand new husband, the picture of masculine arrogance up to that moment, found himself unable to look directly at her.

'Of course,' he mumbled at the napkin.

'Then I'm glad,' Valeria added. 'No matter what we had to go through, it was probably worth it.'

'Probably,' he muttered. It was a curious reaction from a man like him, and the thought nagged at Valeria for the rest of the evening as she helped Mabel and Harry through the clean-up, and struggled tiredly off to bed.

A hot shower did something to rebuild her spirits. Veiled in a wreath of steam, blush-red all over, she wiped a space clean on the mirror, took a deep breath, and did her best to look like a *femme fatale*. The woman who peered back at her wore a look of perpetual amazement, an innocence that was true, but beyond her years entirely. She put one hand on her hip and essayed a little wiggle. Nothing sexy about that! she sighed disgustedly. Her hands cupped her breasts. She took another deep breath and turned sidewise. And nothing sexy there, either, girl! My daughter's better equipped in that department than I'll ever be!

Disgustedly, she slipped on her ancient towelling robe and went out into the bedroom. Mabel had come through again. The newspapers for the last four nights were piled up on her bed.

Her hair-dryer buzzed in one hand as she worked it around over her mass of hair. With the other hand she sorted out the papers in proper order, until the one from the day of the riot was on top. Her fingers were still a little damp, and it was hard to sort through the pages to get to the comics. When she did, Hagar did not disappoint her.

So, with a chuckle, and a desire not to anticipate the *next* night's strip, she leafed through the pages of Tuesday's paper randomly, stopping here and there to read an ad, or look at a picture, until finally she folded her way back to the first page. And a little block in the lower right-hand corner caught her eye. 'New Appointment,' the headline said. And the story began with, 'Not three hours after he had taken the oath of office as a judge on the Superior Court of the Commonwealth, Judge Bartholomew Thomas was busy bailing his wife and daughter out of the hands of the Plymouth police, the aftermath of an anti-nuclear demonstration that ended up in a riot. In the most unusual swearing-in ceremony yet experienced at the State House, the new judge was administered the oath of office in an elevator in the Capitol building as he rushed to rescue his family.'

'And he never said a word about it,' Valeria mused, a tiny smile on her face. A smile that gradually changed and hardened into a glare as she went back over the sentence in the article. Not three hours *after* he had taken the oath—on the day of the riot, he had already been sworn into office *before* I ended up in the hospital and Maria ended up in jail. *Before!* Before! There was no *need* for all that agony—or for the wedding!

With her head in an uproar, she snatched up the paper and brought it close for a check-up. The words did not change. Her Brewster temper rose—and went right through the roof. Barefoot, clad only in her towelling robe, the newspaper rattling in hands that shook under her primordial anger, she slammed her way out of her room and down the hall.

His bedroom door was closed, but there was a thin crack of light appearing at the bottom. She clenched her fists at her breasts, sniffed away the two tears that were forming, one in each green eye, and slammed her way inside without knocking.

Bart Thomas was sitting up in bed, with pillows stacked behind him, a book in hand. A light sheet covered him from the waist down, and a big grin covered him from the waist up. Valeria stalked over to the foot of his bed, ready to kill. 'You—you——' she stuttered angrily, waving the newspaper in front of her.

'Why, what a pleasant surprise.' His grin grew wider. 'I'm always glad to welcome my wife to my bedroom.' Why does he look so much like a wolf? Val asked herself. But her anger drove her on. She rattled the newspaper at him.

'It says here,' she managed to get out, 'that you were confirmed four days ago, Bart Thomas! *Four days ago!*'

'Don't shout—there's a good girl,' he returned rather mournfully. 'I hadn't expected you'd be the kind of wife who read back issues of the paper.'

'*Four days ago,*' she roared at him. 'How could you do this to me? There was no need for the wedding. No need at all. Oh, God, how could you?' There were no tears. She was too angry to cry. He needed assassinating, not tears—but she hadn't brought a weapon of any kind with her.

'There was every need of a wedding,' he said softly. So softly that she had to curb the dry sobs that were shaking her, or miss what he was saying.

'What do you mean—every need?' she asked. His grin was gone. She had never seen him look so solemn—and so tentative. He was worried about her reaction, and that worried her. She repeated her question.

'I've been trying to find a way to get you to marry me for the past five weeks,' he sighed. 'Valeria, I know it was a rotten trick to play on you, but I've loved you since that first day we came here, when you and Amelé stood side by side at the pool—and *she* came out second best.'

The newspaper slipped from Valeria's nerveless fingers as she tried to make sense out of what he was saying. She made one stab at her dry eyes with a knuckle, and then crossed the fingers on both hands. 'You—you what?' she stammered.

'I fell in love with you,' he repeated, more firmly this time.

'And you tricked me because——' she started out slowly.

'Because I couldn't find any other way to convince you to go through with it,' he admitted. 'Every time I brought up the subject you roared at me. Now, have I done such a terrible thing?'

Both her hands fell to her sides. She straightened her back, brushed her long fall of hair back over her shoulders, and thought. It was hard to believe. He had loved her all this time—and *she* hadn't realised she loved *him* until the moment that the minister said——

'No,' she said. It came out as a gruff little squeak of protest. 'No,' she repeated more firmly. 'You didn't do a bad thing. I love you too, Bart.' There was something about that last sentence that sounded so—wistful—even to her own ears.

'Then there's no need for recrimination?' There it was
again, that wish-bearing question. This big, assured, arrogant man lying on the bed in front of her was not all
that assured, after all.

'Well,' she said, hurrying to get the words out, 'I'm
not exactly in love with that platonic marriage idea.' His
grin was back, wider than before, if that were possible.
His big white teeth gleamed at her.

'I've never been crazy about that myself,' he agreed.

'Well, then—it's up to the man to do something about
it,' she told him. He nodded, and one hand reached down
to flip the sheet entirely from his body. 'Like that?' he
asked.

Valeria swayed in the wind of emotion that gripped
her. Even virgins have dreams, she told herself, but this
was the first man she had ever—oh, my! Her fingers
fumbled at the belt that held her robe together. It required no urging, but fell from her shoulders to huddle
around her feet, leaving her an alabaster statue, posed
in the light from his bedlamp, as God had made her.

'Come here, wife,' he commanded.

'Mabel said a bride needed more sustenance than usual,'
Valeria giggled. The big clock in the hall had just struck
two in the morning, and she was feeling battered and
beautiful.

'No need to rush off,' he chuckled, pulling her down
on his shoulder again. 'I love that hair—and those eyes—
and those——' His fingers caressed her sensitive and
tender skin.

'You think you're Superman, don't you?' she said
fondly. 'I'll bet you a nickel that you can't——'

By dawn she owed him fifteen cents, was thoroughly
worn out, and had never spent a better night in all her

young life. But there was no way he was going to make it twenty. His eyes were half closed. He was not asleep, but not far from it, either.

'What are we going to do about Maria?' he asked suddenly.

'Do? Why should we do *anything*?' Valeria rolled in his direction, teasing him with the tips of her pert little breasts. Her pert, tender little breasts. The great conquering male managed a grunt of protest. 'You have a headache?' she coaxed.

'Damn woman,' he grumbled, but his heart wasn't in it. 'You're not—upset—by having Maria around?'

Val laid her head back on her pillow. The old cliché was true. There's no use beating a dead horse, she told herself. But maybe with a little rest there's resurrection? She turned her head and examined her man speculatively. 'Maria is our eldest child,' she told him softly. 'And think how nice it will be to have a built-in babysitter for the rest of them when they come along.'

'Them?' he asked in a mutter that presaged his slipping over the edge.

'Them!' she returned very firmly.

'Then I'd better get some sleep,' he mumbled. 'I'm going to need my rest.' And he was gone.

Valeria sat up in bed, the sheet slipping down to her knees. My man, she thought. He was breathing through his mouth—not snoring, but breathing heavily. His facial muscles had relaxed, leaving him wearing that appealing, boyish look that she so much loved. Mrs Valeria Thomas. He deserves me. A smile traced across her lips. Gran would have loved him. So do I. Platonic marriage, hah!

The sun poked one little finger of light through the open window, and the finches began their cacophony of welcome. She leaned over his sleeping form protectively, brushed the lock of hair back off his forehead, and gently kissed the spot. The smell of roses flood the air. Slowly, so as not to disturb him, she settled back down, close up against him, her head on his shoulder, said a short prayer of thanks, and joined him in sleep.

# ANNOUNCING . . .

# *The Lost Moon Flower*
## *by Bethany Campbell*

### Look for it this August
### wherever Harlequins are sold

HR 3000-1

They went in through the terrace door. The house was dark, most of the servants were down at the circus, and only Nelbert's hired security guards were in sight. It was child's play for Blackheart to move past them, the work of two seconds to go through the solid lock on the terrace door. And then they were creeping through the darkened house, up the long curving stairs, Ferris fully as noiseless as the more experienced Blackheart.

They stopped on the second floor landing. "What if they have guns?" Ferris mouthed silently.

Blackheart shrugged. "Then duck."

"How reassuring," she responded. Footsteps directly above them signaled that the thieves were on the move, and so should they be.

*For more romance, suspense and adventure, read Harlequin Intrigue. Two exciting titles each month, available wherever Harlequin Books are sold.*

INTA-1